Do you trust your memory?

More titles by Nick Kolakowski

Love & Bullets

Boise Longpig Hunting Club

Rattlesnake Rodeo

Maxine Unleashes Doomsday

Absolute Unit

Payback is Forever

Hell of a Mess

BEACH BODIES

By

Nick Kolakowski

BEACH BODIES

Text copyright © 2022 Nick Kolakowski

Published by Final Round Press

Cover by A.A. Medina

First Printing 2022.

To the stonks, S. and B. —

ONE

Alec moved to Kyiv because someone on a Reddit forum told him it was a cryptocurrency paradise, money raining from the sky if you had the coding skills, but the only thing raining from the sky was Russian artillery and that's how he ended up on Julia's couch with an ass full of shrapnel.

Well, not *her* couch. It belonged to the secretive billionaire who owned this luxury doomsday bunker on a remote beach. The couch was upholstered in exotic animal hide and cost more than her annual salary. Over the past seven days of his stay, Alec had coated a sizable percentage of its expensive fur with Cheez Kneez crumbs, evidently not caring about her need to keep this place pristine as a museum.

Every day, we expect you to mop everything down, the recruiter told her. *Every day.* Just in case a thermonuclear war popped off on short notice and the billionaire needed to take cover here, along with his trophy wife and screeching kids and social-media manager and whoever else had slimed their way into his entourage. Because when the sky is on fire and people are crisped to ash and you need to murder another CEO for a private jet out of San Jose airport, the last thing you want to see when you walk into your multi-million-dollar bunker is a stain on the floor or a dirty glass in the sink.

Or a cabinet empty of Cheez Kneez.

"What kind of tech stack you think this bad boy is rocking?" Alec asked, lying on his side to spare his perforated ass-cheek.

"Tech stack?" Julia asked from the doorway. She was dressed in what she referred to as Bohemian Chic, her hair tucked beneath a sweaty bandana and her body wrapped in an oil-stained peasant dress. She had a wrench in her left hand, having just returned from whaling on a metal box outside that contained a tiny drone.

"Like, I know it's a pretty sweet broadband connection for the middle of nowhere," he said, pausing to chew another orange Cheez Kneez. "The guy's got to have some pretty powerful hardware running, right? Ton of GPUs?"

"Why?"

"Because maybe I can get some mining done," he shrugged like it was the most obvious thing in the world. "Nothing too heavy, but there are some new coins I want a stake in. What's with the wrench? You gonna kill me?"

"Not yet," she said, grinning like it was a joke, but the idea of slamming the heavy metal tool through his forehead had a warped appeal. Even if she didn't really want to kill him, she had grievously underestimated how quickly he would outwear his welcome.

"Then what's it for?"

"There's a surveillance drone that launches from a box near the front door. It's tiny. Flies up automatically whenever anything trips the sensors around the property. Except right now, it keeps trying to fly but it's telling me the box is jammed closed."

"Wait. There's someone out there?" He slid upright, still gingerly resting on his good ass-cheek, so he could peer out the floor-to-ceiling window to his right. The bunker was mostly above ground, a cluster of concrete blocks embedded into the rocky flank of a massive hill, and through the glass they had an epic view of the flawlessly azure ocean beyond a screen of scrubby trees. It was maybe a hundred yards to the shoreline but the glass was thick enough to block the rhythmic crunch of waves.

"I don't think there's anyone for fifty miles around," she said. "The system's sensitive, they told me. Picks up big birds, wild pigs, whatever else might be out there. One of the house monitors," she pointed to the black screen embedded into the doorway, "kept saying 'drone release error.'"

"And you're trying to free it by hitting it?"

"Look, if I could free it up by typing out some code, I would, but I'm not a nerd, okay?" she waggled the wrench at him. "Maybe you could fix it. Make yourself useful."

"I'm injured," he whined. "I got shrapnel in my ass."

"Hasn't curbed your appetite."

"Part of the healing process." His hand disappeared into the jumbo snack bag on the cushion beside him. "Fats, proteins, sugars, it's what you need to knit the muscle back together. Get stronger. Besides, there's not much else to eat, unless you count those crap bars as 'food.'"

Those "crap bars," wrapped individually in foil and stacked in the kitchen's deep cabinets, mixed soy protein isolate, sunflower oil, amino acids, and vitamins and minerals. Flavors included chocolate, vanilla, or (God help them all) 'umami.' One of the billionaire's Silicon Valley friends, too busy to eat while coding late into the night, had created this culinary horror and marketed it under the name "F00d1." The idea failed miserably, and

Julia assumed the billionaire had arranged to fill the bunker with the unsold product, which had no expiration date.

"It's not the worst-tasting thing," she said, unsure why she was defending tech bro capitalism. "It's a little earthy, I guess, but it's nutritious."

"We have no idea what's really in those appetizingly greenish-brown bars, label or no. With Cheez Kneez, I know we got, let's see," he consulted the nutrition panel on the back of the bag, "'enriched corn meal, corn syrup, natural and artificial flavors, canola oil, synthetic cheddar cheese.' Anyway, what about this dude's tech stack? My laptop got fried, remember."

When he first arrived at the bunker, he'd shown her photos of the MacBook Pro in question, its aluminum shell riddled with jagged holes. If he hadn't slipped the laptop into his backpack before an ill-advised sprint across the street to a coffee shop at exactly the wrong moment, the shrapnel from the artillery shell would have carved out his spine in addition to spearing his ass. She knew the bunker had ten laptops stacked like poker chips in the locked maintenance room off the courtyard, but damned if she would give him the code for the door—the second he used one to connect to the internet, it would probably light up a security dashboard in the billionaire's office like a Christmas tree, and her professional fucking would commence in earnest.

Her recruiter was fine with visitors, at least after they ran a CIA-caliber background check on Alec. *JUST MAKE SURE TO CLEAN*, the email had read. *GUESTS LEAVE **NO** MESS.* But she wasn't going to risk her job so Alec could mine FartCoin or whatever.

"Not a chance in hell," she said, offering Alec a sunny smile. "I got to keep working, so just do the normal thing and rot your little brain with whatever's streaming, okay? If you want to make yourself useful, you could help me figure out this drone thing."

"Fine, whatever. I'll help out more in a day or two," he said, retrieving the small silver remote that powered the enormous flatscreen bolted to the opposite wall. He'd been watching a mindless action movie when she popped her head in, but during their conversation the screen had reverted to sleep mode, displaying a decades-old black-and-white photograph of the ocean view outside. Nothing had changed in all that time, except for some undulations in the shoreline, which didn't surprise her at all, given the remoteness. To reach this place, you needed to fly into the regional airport a few islands away, then charter a boat small enough to negotiate the reef, then actually find the bunker amidst the shadowy inlets and crumbling volcanic hills.

While she was here alone, she tried to avoid thinking about injuries. If she fell and broke her leg, how long would it take to reach the nearest good hospital? Seven or eight hours? Having Alec around didn't make things much better—what if he had an infection or something?

"I'll hold you to that," she said, but he pressed the 'play' button on the remote and her last two words were lost in a multi-speaker rattle of machine-gun fire, capped by an enormous explosion. Onscreen, Stallone cracked a dude's neck.

Trying to ignore her creeping anxiety, she retreated deeper into the bunker. The main hallway led to wide stone stairs descending to a perfectly square courtyard with gray concrete walls. A frosted-glass skylight three stories above. With the push of a button, the recruiter told her, a steel panel would slide over that aperture, offering protection from anything short of a nuke. Sealing them inside a luxury tomb, Julia thought. Just like the Pharaohs of old. Mummifying in climate-controlled coolness forever and ever and ever.

It wasn't the most comforting idea.

The architect who designed this bunker had intended the courtyard as its heart, the place where the sheltering family would presumably spend their waking hours in fun and conversation, but the space lacked human warmth. Concrete benches ran along the walls at intervals, and the floor was tiled with black and gray squares, like an oversized chessboard. Embedded in the wall to her right was a long fish tank, lit bluely from within. One of her primary jobs was to open the hidden port above the tank once a day and drop a few sprinkles of foul-smelling powder into the water: sustenance for the spiny, iridescent fish shimmering inside.

On her way down the stairs, she offered them the usual greeting: "Hello, fellow prisoners!"

The fish gasped at her in return. She liked to think they recognized her by this point. Probably not, though. Their brains were the size of pencil erasers. Maybe they would have been far happier swimming in the ocean just outside, but she suspected they'd last thirty seconds before a larger fish snatched them up.

From the courtyard, doors to her left and right led to hallways connected to bedrooms, bathrooms, the surprisingly large kitchen. There was a wood-paneled dry sauna and a steam room beside a narrow nook with a gleaming black stationary bike. The ceilings studded with round bulbs meant to simulate natural sunlight, along with black modules she assumed were cameras recording their every move.

She was forbidden from using the master bedroom, which was bigger than her college apartment. The kids' rooms were off-limits, too. Instead, she occupied the space presumably meant for the lowest-ranked member of the billionaire's post-apocalyptic entourage: a concrete box barely large enough to accommodate a double mattress and blonde-wood bedframe, with a single light overhead and a framed print of the pristine Swiss countryside above the headboard.

Before Alec arrived, she slept in one of the front rooms, close to the windows, but she had retreated down here during his stay. If she slept up there, he would likely make assumptions about her feelings. She knew he felt their relationship hadn't been the emotional equivalent of a forty-car highway pileup.

And maybe it wasn't. She'd allowed him to stay here, right?

"Not important right now," she told herself, typing in the code for the steel door to the maintenance room, which was far larger than her bedroom. The tool rack was just inside, and she hung the wrench beside the hammer and the screwdrivers and the pliers and every other tool she was expected to use to keep this place operating. When she applied for the job, she lied and said she was handy, even spun a heartwarming story of summers helping her father work on rebuilding his car engine. Total bullshit. She'd never met her father.

The far side of the chamber was dedicated to tech: laptops, servers, a pair of VR goggles, spare Bluetooth keyboards and tablets and phones still in shrink-wrapped packaging. Amidst those high-tech gizmos, the object on the bottom shelf stood out as an oddity: an oily, sand-crusted chainsaw.

She stepped out of the maintenance room and shut the door. The monitor set into the courtyard wall beeped and flashed to life, its built-in speaker crackling. Oh goody, a rare voice communication from the recruiter, who she imagined was ensconced in a comfortable office far above the streets of Seattle or Los Angeles or Hong Kong.

"We are receiving reports of a drone malfunction," the speaker said. *"Report."*

She waved at the closest ceiling module. Someone was probably watching her. Pricks. "The lid of the box is jammed," she said. "It can't fly out."

A pause, a click, followed by a low humming. *"Take the box apart."*

"But what about the elements?"

"The what?"

"The salt air and humidity and stuff. I leave the drone exposed, it'll break down."

"Put box back together after drone leaves. Use your ingenuity. That's why we hired you, correct?"

I thought you hired me to clean obsessively, she wanted to say. "I'll figure it out."

"Do it now."

"Why?"

"Sensors now indicate multiple movements."

"A herd of…" She struggled to remember the kinds of animals native to this nowhere zone. "Pigs or something?"

The humming again—too long this time. *"Algorithm says possible humans."*

"Out here?"

"Unknown."

"Tourists? Is there a boat or something?"

"Unknown."

Her palms were sweaty. "If they're on foot, the fence will stop them."

"Incorrect."

"No, there's a fence. You told me. It's a mile out, in the scrub."

"There is a fence. They are past it already."

Her pulse thudding in her ears. "What do I do?"

"They are close. Follow protocol from orientation."

Shit, the protocol. She knew what it was—you didn't sign on for an eight-month stint in a place like this without memorizing everything related to your safety. But in her rising panic, she forgot the steps. Shit!

"Nonlethal use is authorized," the speaker said. *"First gun cabinet unlocked."*

A deep thump from the courtyard wall to her left, and the outline of a narrow rectangle appeared in the concrete—a drawer popping free, sliding out to reveal an almost comically large six-shooter nestled in gray foam. In the cutout beside it, a handful of fat red shells. Like the earth itself birthing her a gun.

The fish seemed unimpressed by this latest development.

Her shaking fingers made it hard to load the weapon. "Can you call that private security firm? The rapid response team?"

The speaker crackled—or maybe it was the recruiter snorting. *"If the situation warrants it. Evaluate threat first."*

"Remind me, how long would it take them to get here?" She slipped the last shell into the chamber and slapped the weapon closed. She knew the answer to the question, but the hopeful part of her (the part that refused to die no matter how much of life's shit she took) wanted to hear something different.

"Three hours."

"Great," she said, pressing the weapon against her hip as she scampered up the steps toward the front rooms.

TWO

Alec had turned the television off and climbed from the couch, favoring the leg connected to the uninjured side of his ass. He startled when he saw the gun in her hand. "What the hell?"

"Don't worry, it shoots some kind of pepper ball," she said. "Nonlethal."

"Why are you carrying it?"

"There's something out there. If it's a person, and they don't back off after the first warning, I'm supposed to fire a round at them."

Alec hopped toward her. He had propped a cane against the wall beside the door, an oddly antique-looking number with a curved handle and a tiny bronze skull on the upper shaft. Whenever she saw it, she imagined him picking it off a dead man in the ruined streets of Kyiv, but he'd probably paid a few bucks for it in a thrift store.

"What if they're just lost or something?" he said, grabbing the cane. "Or trying to sunbathe on a deserted beach? You could get sued."

"I'll tell them to leave, first," she said. "Then we'll move to the good ol' ultraviolence."

She was joking about the ultraviolence part. She'd never fired a gun in her life, and the prospect of doing so terrified her. When she signed up for this weird gig in the great nowhere, she assumed the biggest risk was boredom. That she would spend every day cleaning sand and mud from the floors and counters, catching up on her reading, and trying to avoid thinking about the hell-mess she'd left behind in the real world.

Well, maybe the recruiter was wrong. Maybe it wasn't people out there.

If it's not people, what could it be? Friggin' Bigfoot?

What a comforting thought. Imagine the note in her college's alumni magazine, the section devoted to obituaries:

Julia Herbert ('18) *was torn apart by what authorities are now assuming was an unusually large Sasquatch. Although everyone at the school mourns her passing, the physical particulars of her demise left enough DNA evidence to confirm that 'Bigfoot,' long considered a charming myth, actually exists! A cryptozoology chair will be endowed in Julia's honor.*

No. Stop thinking that way, she told herself. You know what happens when your thoughts start spiraling. You need to deal with this, whatever it is. Earn your miserable paycheck.

Spinning on her heel, she moved across the hallway to the other front room, almost identical in its layout. An enormous wooden table stretched across the space, its far side stacked with board games like chess, checkers, Monopoly, Risk, and weirder ones she'd never seen before: Nut Up, Ninja Poop, Exploding Cows. Under ordinary circumstances, she hated board games, which reminded her a little too much of all those sweaty summer afternoons in the trailer growing up, where the options were either making up new rules for checkers or setting things on fire. Another month or two of living here, though, and she would probably develop a newfound appreciation for buying Mediterranean Avenue or picking up plastic ninja poo without setting off the board's electric buzzer.

She stepped around the table so she could reach the wall beside the window. Tapped the concrete with the side of her hand. A hidden panel slid open, revealing a set of bright red buttons along with a small black speaker. She found the button marked 'OUT,' just like they had taught her during orientation, and rested her finger on it, ready to push. Stared out the window, waiting.

The beach was a wide swath of pristine white sand. At either end, the sand gave way to low ridges of rock and scrub topped by small trees. To her right, beyond the trees, she spied a flash of smooth yellow. It gleamed like plastic in the harsh sunlight before dipping below the ridgeline again.

Her heart slammed against her sternum. Alec's cane scraped the concrete behind her, but she kept her eyes locked on the ridge. The yellow reappeared, moving to the left, toward the water. A glimpse of red behind it.

She took a deep breath, held it until her lungs burned. She pictured her body as an empty vessel filled with toxic-green anxiety; when she exhaled, in a loud rush, the green cloud flowed from her body. She breathed in again, thinking: calm, calm, calm, calm, calm.

Her heart refused to slow.

A flash of blue behind the red. It was three people walking in a line toward the water, probably so they could walk onto this stretch of beach without risking an ankle on the ridge's rocky slope.

She pressed the red button, dipped her head to the speaker, and said: "This—this is private property, okay? You are trespassing. Leave the way you came."

She wasn't sure what would happen next. During the orientation, the recruiter told her about the speakers planted at intervals around the bunker, capable of broadcasting a range of messages and sounds. Except on her walks around the property, she'd seen nothing that resembled a conventional speaker. She envisioned tiny metal buds poking from the sand, plastic stalks hidden in the reeds. Against the immensity of the ocean and dunes and rocky hills, would anyone hear if those devices made a—

"This—this is—"

Her own voice, amplified to Biblical levels, shaking the window, blasting birds into startled flight. She almost screamed. The message rumbled along like a tank advance through Russia, quaking trees along the ridges where she guessed a few speakers were hidden:

"—trespassing. Leave—"

Behind her, Alec cursed and fell to the floor, his cane skittering away, then screamed as the concrete impacted his shrapnel-studded flesh.

"—you came."

The speakers clicked and fell silent. She tried breathing in blue, exhaling green. If any small varmints had the misfortune of hopping near a speaker when her message boomed out, the sound waves had probably liquified them to a pink mist. But what about the people?

She stared out the window, waiting.

No movement along the ridge or the shoreline.

Maybe they had fled.

If so, good. The system worked as intended. If they were day-hikers on a tropical jaunt, they could find their way back to their boat and tell a dandy story about the time they ran into God out in the wilderness. And if they were up to something more nefarious, well, she didn't want to think too much about that. Not yet.

"The fuck?" Alec asked, rising to his feet and retrieving his cane.

"A million dollars of subwoofer," she said, and giggled.

"Fucking hell."

"Well, it drove them off."

"Drove *who* off?"

Another click. Every muscle in her body tensed, ready for another sonic assault. But it was only the recruiter, whispering across a couple thousand miles of fiber: *"They're still out there. Coming closer."*

"Who?" Alec yelled at the ceiling. "Who the fuck is out there?"

"Guest," the recruiter said. *"Do not interfere with protocol, or you'll wish you were back in Ukraine, trying to negotiate that Bitcoin deal."*

"How the fuck did you know about my deal?" Alec yelped.

"Julia," the recruiter said. *"You are to head outside. Direct interdiction with intruders. Or risk immediate termination."*

"Aren't we safer in here?" she asked. "It's a fortress."

"You must ensure property integrity."

"The fuck," Alec muttered. "Isn't this a bunker?"

Yes, but an oddly delicate one. During orientation, as the recruiter's disembodied voice muttered directions through the wireless buds in her ears, Julia had walked to the top of the bunker's hill, where a set of solar panels and a backup generator squatted within a chain-link enclosure, along with a steel hut containing the water filtration system, circuit breakers, and a few racks of electronics. At least, that's what they told her was inside the hut, because she didn't have the key to unlock the gate.

The chain-link was electrified, which wouldn't stop a determined intruder from causing a little mischief, she guessed. And in the grand equation, her safety evidently mattered less than a billionaire's property. Not exactly a shocking revelation, was it?

"Well, fuck me sideways," she said, marching for the bunker's front door. She was still frightened, still too filled with toxic green, but a righteous fury struck matches in her belly. Fuck the billionaire who demanded she put herself at risk. Fuck whoever was outside, refusing to flee despite the wall of sound. The fury would help get her through.

THREE

To the uninitiated, the bunker's front door was the kind of wooden monstrosity you might find in a Medieval castle or a Hollywood mansion trying to imitate a Medieval castle. But as the recruiter explained to her, the wood sandwiched a pane of metal thick enough to absorb a direct hit from a rocket launcher or a bomb. The lock connected to three bolts the size of Julia's forearm. It had more sensors and microchips than most cars.

"You're really going out there?" Alec said, falling behind her as she marched down the short hallway to the front door. "What you going to do, point that gun at them?"

"I guess." Not for the first time, it occurred to her that so many people in this part of the world were armed. She remembered landing at the crappy little airport on the big island and seeing men outside the terminal with pistols shoved down the front of their faded jeans, seemingly unconcerned about the sleepy cops a few feet away. It wasn't all sun and fun down here, and she wasn't ready for a shootout.

"And if that doesn't work?"

"We call for help," she said, opening the door. Despite its weight, it moved easily on its counterbalanced hinges. "There's a rapid response team on the next island. They'll fly in here, I think. Lock this place down."

"Yeah? They'll just drop from the sky like the Navy SEALs? You believe that?"

She spun on him. He was scared, chewing the inside of his cheek, his hands balled into loose fists. During their relationship, he'd burned so much energy playing tough, but underneath all the bravado was a very sensitive boy, one shaken to his core by the artillery in Kyiv.

"Sure, I believe it," she said, feeling a little bad about the lie. "Stay up here."

"Where are you going?"

"Not far," she said, stepping outside. It was cooler than she expected, almost the same temperature as the bunker, for which she was thankful—she tended to sweat, it was one of those genetic things that made her uncomfortable at concerts and parties, and the last thing she wanted was the gun to slip from her moist hands. The tang of salt in the back of her throat, along with a hint of rotting seaweed.

From the front door, a long set of stairs descended to a black-rock path through the low dunes, lined on either side with knee-high sand reeds. She went down, a hand over her brow to block the worst of the sun, scanning the ridge for any movement. Nothing. Were they hiding? Had they turned back?

She followed the path to its endpoint on the beach. She stepped from the rocks and sank to her ankles in the hot sand. She looked over her shoulder. Alec stood by the doorway, his head swiveling as he scanned for intruders. From her new angle, the enormous pale dome of the hill with the large windows set into it, the open door and the stairs beneath, all reminded her of a skull with its tongue lolling out. Not the first time she made that connection. A lonely tomb in the wilderness, a king's home for a thousand years.

She shuddered and slipped the pistol into the oversized pocket of her dress so she could wipe her hands on her hips. Drew the weapon again. She was too exposed here, a lone spot on the pale beach. If the people out there were armed, they could snipe her from the ridge.

She wanted to run back up the stairs, except the prospect of turning her back on the vast emptiness was too frightening. Deep breath—green out, blue in. After however many days of bunker air, sterilized by the next-generation filtration system, inhaling the great outdoors was such an overpowering experience she almost coughed, her throat burning, her tongue thick.

Her heart calmed a little more. Or at least the thudding in her ears was a little softer.

"Hello," she called out—too softly for anyone to hear over the crash of waves.

Something zipped past her ear, and she flinched. A mosquito, probably. They were as big as fighter jets out here.

She tried again, much louder: "Hello! You're trespassing!"

To her right, stones crackled. A flash of yellow rising over the ridge's jagged edge, resolving into a raincoat, its arms shredded, its front flecked with leaves and dark splashes. The face framed by the raincoat's raised hood was pale and baby-smooth, almost like a doll's head. A male of indeterminate age, heavy-set, his massive shoulders sloping beneath slick plastic. The eyes a deep green that reminded her of the Atlantic Ocean in winter, cold depths over a graveyard of shipwrecks.

She absorbed the man's other details: dirty jeans, old hiking boots caked with mud, a faded blue backpack too small for anything other than a day trip. No weapons she could see. He was already descending the ridge, hopping from rock to rock with the agility of a goat, then onto the sand, marching toward her, fifteen yards away, ten, five…

"Stop," she said, raising the pistol.

The man stopped and smiled, revealing small and perfect teeth gleaming in the sunlight like pearls. "Hello," he said. "Was it you with that megaphone? Quite a noise."

"You're trespassing," she said. "I'd like you to, ah, turn around. Leave."

The smile dipped into a soft frown. "I'm afraid I can't do that. We need help."

"Help?"

Two new figures crested the ridge. The larger one wore a red raincoat, also stained and torn. This one was a woman, her face large and square, her red hair chopped down to tufts. Everything in her expression screamed panic, her pupils vibrating, her mouth gaping open.

The woman in the red raincoat had her arms around her companion in a blue raincoat. Well, only parts of it were blue, because an extraordinary quantity of dark liquid had stained its back and sides. Based on how the figure in the blue raincoat was hunched over, arms wrapped around its torso, trembling legs skewed at odd angles, Julia bet the liquid was blood. The lifted hood made it impossible to see the face.

With a titanic grunt, the woman worked her way down the ridge, almost dragging her companion behind her. A small avalanche of pebbles and sand beneath their scrambling feet. That they managed to reach the beach without toppling over was a small miracle.

"Help," said the doll-faced man. "Or my friend is going to die right here, right now."

FOUR

Julia lowered the pistol. She was vaguely aware of Alec shouting something from the steps, but she needed to concentrate on the man in front of her. The man offered her an apologetic smile, as if to say: *Isn't this a fine kettle of shit we're all dunked in?*

"What happened?" she asked.

The women in the red raincoat stopped and twisted her body, levering the figure in the blue raincoat over her hip. The blue hood slipped back, revealing a man's face, the skin yellowed, the thin beard clotted with dark blood. Nostrils bubbling crimson. The coppery funk of warm, raw meat filled the air.

"Boar," said the woman in the red raincoat. Her tone rumbly-deep, like a truck crawling over a gravel road. "A wild boar did this to him, in the brush. An hour ago. Other side of the island."

Julia swallowed hard as her stomach performed a slow, greasy somersault. *You will not vomit*, she told herself. *You're better than that. Stronger.*

"You need to help us," said the doll-faced man. "You need to help us get him inside."

"No," Julia said, shaking her head. "I can't do that."

"You need to," the doll-faced man said, louder. "Or he's going to die."

The man in the blue raincoat groaned and blew a bloody bubble. Despite the beard, he had the smooth skin of someone barely out of their teens.

"There's too many stairs," Julia said. "Get him down on the sand here. We have a first aid kit inside. A good one."

"Oh, bullshit," the woman in the red raincoat muttered, tightening her grip on the blood-slick body. "Gonna let our boy die because she can't stand to get her precious house a *little messy*."

"It's not a house," Julia said. "And it's not mine." She didn't want to turn her back on these people. Ask Alec to get the first aid kit? No, he didn't know where it was kept. Maybe he could come down and watch them while she went for it. Maybe he could do more for this wounded man. He must have learned some combat medicine in Kyiv, right?

The woman snorted. "Just let us in, you soulless brat."

"Hey." The doll-faced man turned to his companion. "Be kind, okay? Remember what we talked about?"

"He's *fucking dying*," the woman snarled, hoisting the man in the blue raincoat like an oversized sack of potatoes. More blood squirted from between the latter's chapped lips and splattered the pristine white sand.

The doll-faced man shifted back to Julia. "We can't treat him out here. We need water. Clean cloth for bandages. All that stuff. Please. Help us."

"Okay," Julia said. "Okay." This mauled dude might not survive a trip up the stairs, but if he did, they could treat him in one of the front rooms. Would the billionaire fire her for bringing a group of strangers inside? Maybe. But what kind of person didn't do everything possible to save a life?

With a guttural wheeze, the woman stooped, looped her elbow behind her bloody companion's knees, and hoisted him off the sand. Her hood slipped back, revealing her scalp beyond her ears, much of it crosshatched with bright pink scars. The tendons in her neck stood out like steel cords as she hugged the kid to her chest and stomped forward.

"When you're inside," Julia told them. "I can call for help. Someone will come." She hoped so. What if the recruiter said no to a boat or helicopter, even with someone bleeding on the expensive furnishings?

"No," the doll-faced man said. "No help."

"I don't—"

"You're not calling anyone."

"What?"

Quick as a rattler, the doll-faced man lunged forward, his huge hand slipping around the barrel of her weapon, his thumb sliding between the hammer and the frame. Their fingers touched, an electric charge like static, his skin as cool as the metal. Her finger twitched on the trigger, click, but the meat of his thumb absorbed the descending hammer's thump.

She tried to yank the pistol away, but his other hand was already on her elbow, squeezing with crushing force, and her fingers spasmed open. He lifted the weapon and she thought he would point it at her next, but instead he popped open the cylinder and dumped the rounds into his palm.

"What the hell?" he said. "These aren't bullets."

"Non-lethal," she said. "Please, it doesn't have to go like this. Please—"

"Non-lethal," he said, and snorted. "Anything's lethal at point-blank range, you know?"

"I don't—"

"No, you don't." The doll-faced man popped one of the rounds into the cylinder and slapped it closed. "You don't have an original thought in your head, do you?"

The crunch of footsteps on the sand. She turned. Alec hobbled across the beach as fast as he could on one good leg, the cane clutched in both hands as if he meant to swing it at the doll-faced man's head, and she wanted to yell at him to back off, to help the massive woman lift the wounded boy up the stairs.

The doll-faced man raised the pistol, squinted down the barrel, and pulled the trigger. A harsh snap almost lost in the ocean's rumble. A red cloud burst on Alec's shoulder. The stinging reek of pepper. Alec slapped his hands over his eyes and screeched before falling to his knees.

Julia's eyes watered, her mouth bubbling with sour saliva. Fuck, is this what tear gas felt like? Or pepper spray? The nerves in her face tingled and itched, itched, itched so bad she wanted to dig her fingernails into her scalp and peel off her skin down to her chin—

"Relax, it'll pass," the doll-faced man said, popping open the cylinder, dumping out the spent round, and reloading the other five. "Now, we're all going inside, and we're going to do our best for our friend. You talk back to me again, I'll shove this gun up your boyfriend's ass and pull the trigger, and believe me, that's way worse than taking one of these to the face. Do you believe me?"

He's not my boyfriend, she wanted to say, but a stranger didn't need to know that. She knelt beside Alec, who had rolled over onto his hands and knees, the better to cough and hack greenish strands of snot into the sand. His eyes red, swelling. She wrapped an arm around his chest, braced his shoulder, and did her best to lift him up, pressing her cheek against his shoulder as she did so. His body shook as he coughed but his heat was comforting, her last anchor as everything spun out of control.

The woman in the red raincoat had almost reached the top of the stairs, her gruesome burden flailing and dripping in her arms. Could the recruiter see them on camera? Would the massive door with all its sensors swing shut before they could cross the threshold?

No. They swept into the bunker, swallowed by shadows.

"Let's move," said the doll-faced man. "And remember what I said: gun, ass, mess. I mean it."

How dare this asshole threaten them? Her eyes stung less already—they must have cheapened out on the chemical in the bullets. Cool tears still trickling down her hot cheeks. Not tears of fear or pain but a rising frustration, the world-famous Julia temper cycling to life.

FIVE

In her junior year of college, Julia signed up for a creative writing class taught by a brilliant but borderline-incomprehensible professor of Russian origin. Pacing at the front of the classroom, the man liked to start off class by hinting at the dark things in his past: cold-water flats, scurrying past police checkpoints, writing tentacle porn under a pen name. For his first assignment, he asked his students to write a flash fiction piece, nine hundred words or less. Preferably much less. And autobiographical, if you please.

Unlike the other students, Julia didn't like writing about herself. After agonizing over it for a few days, she stumbled upon a solution: if she described herself through Alec's eyes, it would give her enough psychic distance to get the job done. She imagined how he felt about their third date, the sexy one that still made her stomach tingle whenever she thought about it, which was often. When she finally mustered up the courage to sit in the campus library with her notebook and jot the story down, she also opted to use the second-person perspective, because the Russian said it was "brave" and more likely to earn a higher grade. She needed the 'A.'

She submitted:

*The overhead lights dim and the projector above the bar
snaps on, and the gloom is your excuse to press close to
the girl with the butterfly tattoo on her left hand. You
have been circling each other for weeks: a glimpse in the
coffee-shop line, a fingerwave through the subway train's
smeared window, a coffee date, a dinner date. Now she
leans against the exposed brick wall opposite the bar and
you slip behind her, the front of your jacket brushing the
back of hers. She says nothing, but acknowledges your
presence by pushing backwards, once, slowly, to grind
her soft warm ass against your hardness. On the sheet
pinned to the window for a screen, a Lady swoons in
Valentino's embrace. This is the moment for you to lean
forward, to say something sweet, but her cool pale hand
is already in movement: looping backward around her
hip, working your zipper with brisk efficiency. Her other
hand reaches beneath her jacket, to the hem of her short
stretchy skirt, which she lifts in the back to reveal a
breathtaking lack of underwear. The crowd around you is
drawn into the silver shadows of* A Sainted Devil,
*unaware of this other, minor devilry: the hand slipping
you forward, up, moving slowly, faster, faster still.
Breathing teeth-gritted into the back of her neck, her
raven hair smelling of roses and cigarettes. Her other
hand with its brightly inked* Lepidoptera *moves yours*

45

under her suede jacket, to the soft heft of her left breast.
Her pupils reflect in miniature the Big V and Nita
Naldi, perfect ghosts floating aloof through the room.
Fire and wet down both your thighs, shaky-kneed
against gritty brick, her breath a warm roar in your ear:
"I've collected you."

The Russian gave her a B. "Good work harnessing the feminine mystique," he wrote at the bottom. "Next time, write from your point of view."

After much internal debate, she decided to let Alec read it. She found him in his dorm room, wiring together electronics into a mega-computer he claimed would mine Bitcoin with brutal efficiency. He was too busy with his wiring to look up, so she decided to read it aloud. That's what writers did, right? Stand before the microphone in cafés and pour out their little hearts to the world?

She read it to his back, haltingly at first, but gaining speed as she described their fumbling before the altar of a lovingly restored Rudolph Valentino movie. She was remembering his hot breath in her ear, the thrill of expecting someone to see them. Her palms sweaty. Her nipples hardening. She finished, swallowed, and waited for him to respond.

"You're writing smut now?" he asked, still bent over the machine.

She swallowed again. "Um, what did you think?"

He shrugged. "It was okay, I guess. It's not really my thing, you know?"

"Are you offended?"

"Why would I be offended?"

"Because I took liberties with your point of view."

Another shrug. "Doesn't matter."

"It—it does to me," she said, stumbling over the words because she wasn't much of a writer, sure, but she was proud of this utterly pretentious thing she'd created with only her memory and a pen.

He turned and saw her—really saw her. "I'm sorry," he said, and offered the slight smile she loved so much, the one that carved a hint of a dimple in his left cheek.

"It's okay," she said, and meant it. She set the paper on the cheap table beside his bed and knelt beside him and took the tiny screwdriver from his hands and kissed his forehead, then the tip of his nose, then his lips. The sex that followed was divine. For the rest of her life, she would remember looking down and marveling at how their bodies seemed fused together.

Four months later, she cheated on him.

SIX

It was too bad she had double-majored in psychology and political science while Alec earned his degree in software engineering, she thought. If either of them had pursued anything medical-related, they might have known how to patch a boar-mauled torso.

Charging down the hallway, the woman in the red raincoat veered left through the doorway to the front room with the television screen. Through the bunker's front windows, Julia saw her dump the kid in the blue raincoat atop the couch, blood and assorted bits spattering across expensive fur. *Hey, you don't have to worry about the Cheez Kneez dust anymore*, a manic voice yelled from the depths of Julia's mind. *Your ass is so fired.*

Once they reached the top of the stairs, Alec gently pushed her away, then leaned forward so he could hack up another epic load of green snot and drool. She entered the bunker on the heels of the doll-faced man, who waved the pistol over his head in crazed patterns but seemed stunningly calm as he told the woman to get the kid off the couch, please, they needed a hard surface to treat him. The woman growled as she gripped the lapels of the kid's raincoat and hefted him onto the concrete.

49

"Your medical kit, go get it," the doll-faced man said, dropping his blue backpack as he turned to Julia. "Now."

Julia nodded and ran deeper into the bunker, sparing a look back at Alec still at the top of the front stairs, hacking and coughing, his shirt shiny with fluids. She hoped he wouldn't do anything stupid in the next minute. If he did, the doll-faced man would kill them both.

He'll kill you anyway. Kill them first!

No, it was too chaotic. She needed to figure this situation out. Stumbling down the stairs to the courtyard, almost tripping on the concrete risers, she skidded through the doorway to the kitchen. It was a long, narrow space filled with all the latest and greatest gear, from the convection oven to the bright blue mixer gleaming on the concrete countertop like a work of art. She sprinted past all of it to the set of drawers at the far end, beside the imposing chrome slab of the refrigerator. The bottom drawer had a plush blue bag with a giant red cross on its front.

The bag was far heavier than she expected as she slung it over her shoulder by its thick nylon strap. She coughed and her throat burst with pain, another gift from the pepper-spray bullet. She sprinted back to the courtyard, her lungs burning.

From the front rooms drifted a low whining, followed by the doll-faced man's murmur.

She jumped on the first riser, ready to climb the stairs—and stopped.

"Recruiter," she hissed.

No sound from the speakers.

"Call for help," she said. "Please."

Nothing except the fish gawping at her from their tank.

"We need help."

Nada.

"Please."

She sensed—or hoped she sensed—the cameras watching her. What were they doing? She pictured the recruiter or maybe even the billionaire himself watching them from a dozen angles on a single screen, like a digital spider's eye. Maybe they were eating sushi at their desk as the drama played itself out, shifting their gaze from the mayhem long enough to dip a beautiful piece of salmon into their wasabi-spiked soy sauce. Maybe this was the kind of entertainment you enjoyed once you crawled high enough up life's ladder.

No, that wasn't it. Even if they found death and destruction entertaining, she couldn't imagine them liking the prospect of a big mess and a ruined couch. Protect the property at all costs, right? She was surprised they hadn't slammed and locked the front door while everyone was still outside.

"Julia?" Alec called, sounding scared. "Where are you?"

"Coming," she yelled, and, taking a deep breath, charged up the stairs. The scene in the front room had devolved. The kid lay in the center of the space, the raincoat thrown open to expose his body's bounty, his t-shirt and jeans soaked black with blood, his chest a shredded mess. The stench of blood made her nostrils flare, and she swallowed back the acid rising in her hurt throat. The wounds seemed absurdly terminal and yet the kid gasped and burped, his eyes rolling, his fingers twitching.

"You gonna stand there, or you gonna do something?" the doll-faced man said.

"Right," Julia said, dropping the medical kit at her feet and kneeling to unzip it. She wanted Alec beside her, but he had retreated to a corner of the room, as far away as possible from the spreading pool of blood. Flipping open the kit's lid revealed rows of clear bags loaded with everything you might need for a post-apocalypse: bandages, antiseptic, torniquet kits, rolls of tubing and gauze, thermometers and scalpels and scissors and splints and ice packs.

The woman in the red raincoat knelt beside Julia and sorted through the supplies with expert movements, uncovering a clear bag marked 'BANDAGES – ANTIHEMORHAGIC' with two fat bandage rolls inside. Tossing the bag to the doll-faced man, she pulled out a torniquet kit and tore it open with her teeth, the nylon belt spilling out.

Julia was close enough to smell the woman's deep-woods funk, mixed with something else she couldn't quite place over the blood-stench filling her head. Like the sweet rot when you cut open a normal-looking fruit, only to find black pulp and small, squirming bugs.

The doll-faced man opened the bandages and wove them around the wounds on the kid's torso, sliding one hand beneath the spine so he could lift the kid a few inches. The kid hissed through red-smeared teeth, his back leaving the floor with a moist sucking sound.

"I know it's hard," the doll-faced man said. "But you just got to grin and bear it."

In the corner, Alec barked weird laughter.

The doll-faced man grinned at Alec. "We got real claws for alarm here."

Alec's laughter rose in volume and pitch until it sounded like an engine whining up an incline. He tilted forward, his hands on his knees,

53

and the laughter mutated to a hacking cough, deep and rattling. Julia shifted, ready to rush over and help him—and Alec spewed a firehose of green vomit across an ultra-expensive couch already saturated with blood and Cheez Kneez dust.

There goes the resale value! she thought.

Ignoring Alec's spewing, the woman in the red raincoat gripped the kid's left ankle, stretching his mangled leg out. The calf five inches below the knee was almost completely torn away from the bone. She wrapped the torniquet a few inches above the wound and twisted the attached windlass, the blood slowing from a broken-faucet gush to a gentle seep.

Julia felt warmth on her knees. Looked down at the pool of blood soaking into her dress. How could any human being bleed this much? It was insane, so insane her mind refused to process it. Standing, she retreated to Alec's side (making a point of sidestepping the spatters of drying vomit on the floor) and watched as the doll-faced man and the woman mummified the kid in bandages already soaking through.

The doll-faced man looked at Alec. "What blood type are you?"

"O negative," Alec croaked, wiping his mouth with the back of his hand, and of course he would know that—like every other engineer and cryptocurrency miner in their shared orbit, he had gone through a "body hacking" phase where he obsessively recorded everything about his meat-sack, from the calories eaten per day to how many minutes he spent in REM sleep. He could probably rattle off his cholesterol stats if you threatened him, which the doll-faced man seemed perfectly ready to do.

"Then get down here," the doll-faced man said, shifting sideways so he could reach into the medical bag. "You're a donor today."

The woman made a guttural sound deep in her throat and said, "Is that a good idea? You don't know what's in there."

The doll-faced man yanked tubing and a sterile pack of needles from a clear pouch. "I'm aware. But it's not like we have a choice. Not if we want to keep him on this side of the soil."

Julia took Alec's cold hand and squeezed gently. His eyes on her, vibrating with fear.

"If it's any comfort," the doll-faced man continued. "I'm not giving you a choice. Get down here and roll up your sleeve."

Alec did as ordered, stretching out his left arm so the doll-faced man could tap a vein with a thick needle connected to a clear tube. Another needle at the tube's far end plugged into the dying kid's left arm. Alec's dark blood rushed down the tube and the doll-faced man bent forward to squeeze Alec's arm, his thumbs sinking into the pale flesh.

Julia looked for the gun, spotted it in the pocket of the doll-faced man's raincoat. Too difficult to grab it from here. Was there a scalpel in the medical bag? Something sharp she could use? She didn't like the idea of trying to fend off these two weirdos with a tiny blade or needle, but this bunker had other options, yes? Like the chainsaw. Or the blades in the kitchen, sharp and deadly.

While everyone seemed distracted, she backed out the door. The doll-faced man yelled something she couldn't hear over a loud buzzing in her ears. She accelerated to a run in the hallway, descending the steps to the courtyard three at a time. She imagined the little cameras in the ceiling tracking her, the sleek heads in Los Angeles or London or Singapore bent over monitors, debating how to help her through this predicament.

Stopping in the courtyard, she said, "You have to help us."

No response from the walls.

"Why aren't you answering me?"

Nothing.

"It's your property here, remember?"

Nada.

"Fuck," she said, and slammed the side of her fist into the nearest wall. As if hoping it would magically eject another gun into her hands. No such weapon was forthcoming, so she marched through the doorway to the kitchen. The top drawer beside the sink held a variety of expensive knives. Even better, she remembered it also held a big cleaver.

Oh, you'll chop them up now?

I have no idea what I'm doing, she snapped at the gremlin in her skull. But it's better than doing nothing, am I right? If these people mean to kill us—and there's every chance of that—I might as well go down fighting.

You've never killed anyone in your life!

You're never too young to start.

You cry when you kill mice!

Shut up. Shut up. Shut up. Shut up. Shutupshutupshutupshutup—

Her memory was right about the cleaver, which featured a seven-inch blade and a pebbled grip. Perfect for severing chicken tendons, crushing garlic, or slamming through an intruder's skull. Holding it in her right hand, she marched back to the courtyard—and stopped.

The doll-faced man stood at the bottom of the steps, pointing the revolver at her.

"I think we got off on the wrong foot," he said. "My name's Kurt. I'm not here to kill you. Our friend up there just died, but don't worry about it. You got anything to eat?"

SEVEN

They ate in the courtyard. Julia brought out two bags of Cheez Kneez along with a plastic crate of those weird, foil-wrapped food bars. The woman in the red raincoat—she said her name was Moira—sat on the floor and unwrapped a bar with the caution of a bomb-disposal expert picking apart a landmine, pausing every few seconds to sniff it.

"Moira, it's fine," Kurt told her through a mouth full of mushed Cheez Kneez. "It's dead, it can't hurt you."

"It smells like nothing," Moira said, pausing to touch the tip of her tongue to a corner of the bar. "Isn't that weird?"

"It's the miracle of science," Kurt said. "Just accept that and choke it down. We need the calories."

Kurt had the snack bag squeezed between his thighs, used his left hand to reach into it every few seconds for another orange curl. His right hand held the revolver, the barrel pointed at the floor, but Julia believed he was prepared to do terrible things with the remaining pepper rounds if she tried anything. Whenever he moved, the dried blood on his raincoat crackled and popped.

"We're sorry about your friend," Alec said from the far corner, where he lay on his good side, his own snack bag tucked into his elbow. He looked like a vampire victim, his cheeks waxy, his forehead shiny with sweat. How much blood had they drained from him? At least he appeared mostly recovered from the pepper spray bullet.

Kurt nodded. "Thank you."

"Any chance someone could go up and grab my cane?" Alec said. "I don't get why you didn't let me bring it down here."

"For our safety," Moira said.

"What are you doing here?" Julia asked. At Kurt's prompting, she'd returned the cleaver to the shelf and helped herself to a flavored water from the fridge. According to the bright font on the bottle's front, the flavor in question was *Blackberry Strawberry Blast!*, but she thought it tasted like ink. Maybe the taste was the side effect of the adrenaline and other fear-juices curdling in her veins.

"There was a boar," Moira said. "It was right next to us, but we didn't see it until it was too late. It… rammed its horns through Kelby's chest. Just crushed it. Then his leg. Horrible."

"Never seen a boar like it," Kurt said, and shuddered. "Really big. Looked weird."

"I'm sorry to hear that," Julia said, wondering if the cameras were recording them despite the recruiter's silence. Yes, undoubtedly. But why the silence? Maybe an incursion meant they wrote off the bunker and everything in it.

"We've been trying to find this place," Kurt said. "We've been out there for three weeks, going from island to island, hiking in circles mostly. Sweating our balls off, as you can probably imagine." He gestured at the t-shirt and jeans beneath his raincoat, the worn hiking boots with the shredded soles.

"Why are you dressed like that?" Julia asked. "Doesn't seem like the right clothing for this part of the world."

"It's all we have," Moira said, sounding bitter. "You don't give up perfectly good jeans, or a raincoat. I wanted to turn back days ago, but Kurt here, he just had to be right. Had to be a *man*."

"This is ridiculous. There's a body upstairs. We need to call the police." Alec said, before turning to Julia. "Can you ask the manager to call the cops?"

"Which manager?" Kurt asked, tightening his grip on the pistol.

"There's a manager for this building," Julia said. "She's available on speaker. The woman who recruited me, actually."

"This job pay well?" Kurt asked.

She smirked. "At least the rent's free."

"What'd they tell you about this place?"

"It's a bunker. A really nice one. Why were you looking for it?" Escape wasn't impossible, she decided. Get out, hide Alec in the scrub or behind a dune. Run for help. She had done cross-country in high school and college, never championship-level but good for ten or twelve miles at a seven-minute-mile pace. She could loop around to the gravel road connecting this place to the dock, and then—

Then what? There was no resupply boat, nobody else on this island. And she couldn't trust the recruiter to send that rescue team, which left her with exactly jack shit.

"How did you get here?" she asked, trying to sound casual. "A boat or something?"

Kurt glanced at Moira and smirked. "She's so sneaky."

"We swam," Moira said, and chuckled. "Just paddled across the water."

"Nah, let's not kid around with her." Kurt's eyes widened in mock amazement. "We flew. With our arms."

"Forget it," Julia said. They must have a boat, she thought. It's the only reasonable explanation. And I bet it's at the dock or nearby. If I can find it, I can get away from here, find help. Except what if they found Alec while she was gone?

They'd probably hurt him, that's what.

The thought of him in pain made her lungs tight. Wasn't that funny? After all the crap they'd been through—the cheating on both their parts, the fighting, her creeping annoyance with his life choices—she still had this raw feeling for him.

"You're not calling that manager," Kurt said. "You're not calling anyone."

Moira leaned to her right and, with a deep retching sound, ejected a green, chewed-up mess onto the concrete.

"That's disgusting," Kurt snapped at her.

"It's *gross*," Moira whined.

"I ought to make you eat it again," Kurt said. "Maybe I will later, just for fun."

"Sorry. I'm sorry. I apologize." Moira frowned and bent her face close to the cooling muck. Studied it, the tip of her tongue extending between her lips.

"You know what to do," Kurt said.

Moira lapped it up like a dog.

A cold shiver down Julia's spine, followed by a white-hot flare of anger. How dare this fucking man humiliate this lady, she thought. Perhaps it's an opportunity. If Moira fears or hates him, I can use that. Get on her good side, convince her to help.

Moira's cheeks flushed bright red as she flicked her tongue over the last greasy smear. Her breathing heavy. Like she was getting off on it.

I'm not one to kink-shame, Julia thought. I've done my share of perverted shit, but damn, that's a pretty fucking weird fetish. More to the point, maybe Moira isn't an unwilling partner here.

Losing interest in Moira's cleaning routine, Kurt turned to Alec and said, "What happened to you?"

"How far you want to go back?" Alec said.

"I mean what's wrong with your leg?"

"I was in Ukraine." Alec twisted on his hip and raised his shirt a few inches, revealing the skin mottled yellow and purple with bruises. "Took some shrapnel in my hindquarters."

"Ukraine, huh?" Kurt nodded. "We were in this laundromat and a kid with a laptop showed me some footage from the war. He said it was OSINT, which I guess stands for 'open-source intelligence.' It's a bunch of nerds who spend all day on social media, finding battlefield footage, then comparing it to other stuff. They try to create the most accurate maps of what's going on."

"That's just TikTok," Alec said. "I saw real violence. You can't imagine what it was like."

"Considering I'm covered with my friend's blood, I'm pretty sure I have a taste," Kurt said, his stare hardening. "Plus, you have no idea where I've been, what I've been through. I'm my own therapist, and I'm very expensive, you understand?"

Alec shrugged. "Sure?"

"Sure, okay." Kurt said. "I've even been to Ukraine. Not during the war there, of course. I was on my way to Siberia, on a little mission, thought I'd stop by to check out what they had to offer. Nice place. Anyway, back to the laundromat, where this kid is showing me all this footage, I guess the Ukrainian soldiers have those cameras they clip to their helmets, the same ones the skateboarders and the surfers use to show off their stunts. You can watch them attack those big Russian convoys of trucks and tanks."

"I saw one of those convoys," Alec said. "When they were evacuating me. It was all burned up. Dead Russians in the road."

"I'm not surprised. You line up like that on an open road, all that ammunition and fuel, you're going to get hit. If the Ukrainians had anything resembling a huge air force, they probably would have done it right on the first day of the war. If I was a pilot, and I saw the enemy had an obvious setup, let me tell you, I'd be hard as a towel rack to just fly straight over it, do some serious damage."

"What mission?" Julia asked.

Kurt turned to her. "Excuse me?"

"You said you were on a mission. What are you, a spy? A soldier?"

"Oh, none of the above," Kurt said, chuckling as if he'd never heard anything so absurd. "You're on a need-to-know basis, and you don't yet need to know." Shifting to Alec again: "Those Russians lining up like that on the road, you think it was deliberate?"

"I think it was a traffic jam," Alec said. "You have one little road that'll support the weight of those vehicles, hundreds of tons rolling through, your logistics are a mess, and the next thing you know, you're in a line twenty miles long."

"Maybe." Kurt hummed. "I've been to Russia, too. Those people aren't dumb. I mean, they don't have a higher proportion of morons than anywhere else on Earth. But sometimes it's the smartest people who do the dumbest things. And I bet some very smart cookies planned that invasion."

"Maybe," Alec said. "But all I saw was a bunch of wrecked tanks."

"How long were you living there? I mean, before the invasion."

"Not long. Maybe three weeks."

"And where'd you live?"

"Why?"

"I like Kyiv. I'm just curious."

Julia side-eyed Moira, who sat on her haunches, still flushed, offering the room a Mona Lisa smile. Beneath her blood-stiff raincoat, Moira seemed like a dense pillar of muscle, more than strong enough to crush someone in a fight.

"On Prorizna and Khreschatyk," Alec said. "Right on the corner there."

"Oh, near the little red bar?" Kurt's eyebrows shot up. "Or the bar with that brick front, rather? They played good jazz there."

Alec shrugged. "Sure."

"You know the one I mean?"

Alec dug out a fresh handful of Cheez Kneez and took his time chewing. Swallowed. "I sure do," he said. "I don't think I went in, though."

Kurt chuckled.

"What's so funny?" Alec asked.

Kurt shook his head. "You didn't live on Prorizna. Or Khreschatyk, for that matter."

"Didn't I just say I did?"

"There's no bar like that around there."

"Sorry, I was just trying to be agreeable." Alec wiped at his brow. "But I really did live there. I had a little apartment above a vape shop, then there was a shoe store right there. I can't remember every bar."

"How much did you pay in rent?"

"A couple hundred bucks. American."

"Alec," Julia said. "What's going on here?"

"Nothing," Alec said. "This dude's being weird."

"You've never been to Kyiv." Kurt told him.

Alec slapped his palm against the floor. "Dude, what the fuck. Not only I have been to Kyiv, I brought a bunch of it back with me, right in my ass. You can't argue with shrapnel, okay?"

Kurt turned to Julia. "Whatever he's told you, he's lying."

"He's not," she said. "He sent me texts. Photos. He was all over Instagram about it. Why would he fake it? He wouldn't fake it." Was contradicting a man with a big gun the right thing to do? The sinking feeling in her stomach said it was a terrible one, maybe life-ending. But what choice did she have? Whatever was going on here, she needed to trust Alec.

"Why would he fake it? What an excellent question," Kurt said. "Alec, would you care to illuminate us?"

"I'm not fucking lying," Alec said, quavering a little, and tried to rise on his elbow—stopping when Kurt raised the pistol.

"You're definitely fucking lying," Kurt said. "And the saddest part of you fucking lying is—get ready for this, it's a doozy—you don't even know it. You think you're the hero of your own life, don't you?"

Alec was smart enough to keep his mouth shut. In the electric silence, Julia heard—or imagined she heard—a faint rustling, followed by a gurgle. Like a burst of liquid flowing through the tubes behind the walls.

Moira tilted her head toward the stairs.

"What's up?" Kurt asked, shifting to her.

"Nothing," Moira said. "I think we're okay."

"I'm no hero," Alec said, so low it was almost a whisper. "But I got grit, okay? And there are a lot of experts, real alpha guys, who say grit's all you need to survive."

69

"You remember how you got here?" Kurt asked him.

"Uh, yeah? I flew from Poland to New York to, uh…" Alec shook his head. "I was out of it for a lot of the trip, okay? Heavy pain meds."

"I bet," Kurt said. "I just bet."

Another rustle, louder. Was it coming from the front rooms?

Kurt opened his mouth, as if to reply to Alec's asinine statement, and closed it again. Rose to one knee, his grip flexing on the gun. Moira stood, her hands balled into fists, squinting in confusion or maybe fear.

Was the guy upstairs alive?

No, impossible. Most of the guy's blood was splashed across the concrete, mixed with a healthy portion of Alec's. Kurt and Moira wouldn't have given up trying to save him, not until the guy's heart stopped.

Another rustle.

Alec traded a look with Julia, trying to be subtle about it, and she raised a hand: wait. Kurt was on his feet, holding the pistol in a two-handed grip, Moira behind him. Moira kept lifting her right hand, as if ready to grip Kurt's shoulder, before pulling it back.

A muffled crackle, a groan. A shadow flicked across the concrete wall at the top of the stairs. Julia had thought the events of the past hour had tapped out her adrenaline, leaving her an empty husk, but her body let her know she was badly mistaken: her heart slammed against her ribs like a prisoner with a sledgehammer trying to escape, her breath rushing into tight lungs, her skin tingling. Fight or flight, but what was she fighting? Where could she flee?

The kid in the blue raincoat appeared at the top of the stairs. His shredded clothing still dripping thick blood, but his torso and limbs miraculously healed, pale flesh visible through the tears. His bearded face as beatific as a saint in a church's stained-glass window, the eyes sparkling with inner light.

The kid took a breath so deep it seemed to suck all the oxygen from the bunker, all light from the world, all energy from Julia's limbs. He held it for an eternal second, his wild gaze circuiting the courtyard until it found Julia. An invisible spark jumped the space between them, voltage she felt in her stomach and between her legs.

Raising his arms, the kid bellowed like an ancient demon:

"Let's party, bitches!"

EIGHT

Alec said he didn't mean to cheat on her.

It wasn't like he tripped, fell, and his penis miraculously plunged balls-deep in that cute blonde girl from his Introduction to Game Development class. But it was an accident nonetheless, too many beers in the cavernous campus bar and a girl who was a little too willing to listen to him, really listen to him, you know?

Julia didn't know.

Sitting behind the wheel of her car, she snorted and shook her head and poured every ounce of her willpower into holding back the tears. Alec beside her with his hands curled in his lap, head down, talking through how he boned this classmate like it was the biggest error of all time, worse than plowing a school bus full of nuns into another school bus full of orphans.

Alec was naked.

Alec smelled like sweat and cheap beer and a perfume Julia had once sampled in a store but couldn't quite name. It came in a pink bottle and basic bitches loved it, she remembered. Like the basic bitch standing on the steps of the dorm over there, wrapped in a blanket, her phone clutched in her hand. No doubt recording this for posterity or Insta.

Julia regretted slapping the girl across the face.

She should have full-on punched her instead, right in her perfect little nose. Everybody would have understood—except the campus police and the girl's parents, of course. And Julia had no intention of ending up expelled or at the business end of a rich prick's lawsuit.

"I'm sorry," Alec sniffed. "I just felt so lonely, and you know we've been having problems lately, and…"

"Shut up," she said, locked on the girl on the steps, who continued to pace despite the cold night air and the growing crowd of dorm denizens behind her.

"I'm sorry."

"Shut the fuck up," Julia said, louder. "I ought to make you leave that thing on."

She meant the titanium band at the base of Alec's dong. A cock-ring so tight it had trapped the blood, the veiny skin turning purple around it. It had been the girl's idea, Alec had whined as Julia dragged him from the dorm to the car.

Julia understood the appeal: a ring let you keep a magnificent hard-on for hours. Except now the damn thing wouldn't come off, and it was four hours and counting, and the television ads for boner pills always said call your doctor if your erection didn't soften after that long. After too much time, the blood pooled in the wrong places, forming clots and choking off flesh, putting you at risk of amputation.

"Before you smashed her door in, we were trying to figure out what to do," Alec said, and hissed air through his teeth. "It's all tingly and weird. It *hurts*."

"I can drive you to the campus hospital. That's my act of astounding mercy for this evening, you understand?"

Alec shook his head. "No, please. My parents will get the bill and they'll ask about it, you know, and I'll have to tell them. Can't we go to a store and get some lube or something? It'll slide off."

Julia punched the steering wheel. The honk startled the girl on the steps, driving her back a few feet. "Look," Julia said, determined to focus her vision on anything but Alec, because looking at Alec would ignite a rage that might lead to her tearing out his forcibly engorged member by the root. "You were fucking *cheating* on me, you fucker. And despite that *big fucking fact*, I don't want to see you hurt, okay? And what's happening to you right now, it's ER level, okay? We're not going to just lube that fucker off."

"You cheated on me," he muttered.

"I did. A long time ago. I apologized to you. I tried to make amends." Her hands tightened on the wheel, knuckles white. "You don't get to throw that in my face at this moment. You just fucking don't."

"So, we're even," he said, a little stronger.

"No, because I didn't lie to you about it. I didn't force you to kick in a stranger's door so you could find the truth." The wheel squeaked in her grip. "You said you were *studying* tonight."

"I love you."

"Ah, fuck," she said, and twisted the key in the ignition. The car rumbled to life and she stood on the gas, peeling out in a cloud of vaporizing rubber. She made the mistake of giving the girl on the steps a proud middle finger, which necessitated taking a hand off the wheel. The car skittered out of control, almost smashing into the flank of a parked SUV before she corrected. When she reached the next intersection, she slowed and took a left, toward the hospital.

"I really got to pee," Alec said, wincing as he tapped his fingers against the cock ring. "What if they can't get it off? Will my bladder explode? I'm too scared to Google it."

"We'll be there in a minute," she said, wanting to maintain this thunderhead of anger against him, because that would keep the sadness at bay. Her brain, ever the joker, kept flashing memories of their first night together, back in freshman year, when her roommate was out of town and they had the bed to themselves for what felt like endless hours, trying everything, sliding all over the cheap mattress. The best part right before dawn, when she fell asleep in his arms, feeling protected and safe like never before. Like the world could end and he would somehow make everything okay.

God, she was such a chump.

It was early on a Tuesday night and the ER was mostly empty. They only had to wait twenty minutes before a nurse took them back to the curtained examination area. "I don't know about your tolerance for humor right now," the nurse told them as she snapped on a pair of gloves, "but you're not the evening's first sex toy incident."

"I imagine you get a lot of them," Julia said.

"Like you wouldn't believe. They ought to put posters around campus telling people to not put bottles up their rectums." The nurse bent to examine the titanium ring. "How long ago did you put this on him?"

"I didn't put it on," Julia said.

"Maybe four hours ago," Alec offered, almost hyperventilating as he tilted his head for a better look at his purpling junk. The metal bit into the skin, the veins around it dark and bulging.

The nurse offered Julia a quizzical glance. "Are you two together? Or are you a friend?"

"She's my girlfriend," Alec blurted.

Julia shrugged. Alec was wrong, but it seemed simpler to go with the flow, allow the nurse to concentrate fully on the medical emergency at hand. Except that wasn't all of it, right? The faint tug deep within Julia's gut, like a fishing hook pulling her toward something she didn't want to admit: she still cared deeply for this fucker. Probably always would, no matter what terrible and stupid things he did.

"Okay," the nurse said. "Well, in any case, we have a bit of a complication here. This sex toy doesn't have a hinge, which would make it easier to remove."

"Yeah, I know," Alec said. "But can't you cut it off?"

"It's titanium. We can't just clip it off. We don't have anything strong enough to saw through it."

Alec's lower lip trembled. "You have to help me."

"Maybe we could use one of those—what do you call them—torches that cut through metal?" Julia winked at the nurse. "The ones that shoot sparks and get really hot?"

Alec burst into messy tears, his throat hitching as he sucked down ragged breaths between high-pitched squeaks. The nurse placed a hand on his shoulder, a half-hearted gesture of comfort, before turning to Julia. Beneath the cool professional gaze, Julia sensed the woman trying to broadcast a thought to her: *Really? You're dating this?*

Julia pursed her lips. Something about Alec's tears made that fish hook in her belly tug harder, bringing up emotions she'd rather leave tamped down, thank you very much. She kept thinking about their first bed, rolling around beneath her light blue comforter—

Alec whistled down a fresh lungful of oxygen and blurted, "I love you and I always loved you and I'm so sorry, I'm such a jerk, I did it and

I'm sorry, she didn't mean anything and I'm sorry, I love you, I love you, baby, I love you…"

The nurse rolled her eyes and muttered, "Every damn night."

Julia didn't mean to crack. She didn't. Except something in Alec's voice sent chills up her body, followed by a wave of blooming heat. Her cheeks flushed. Terrifying. Where did this feeling come from? Did she really want this? But the rational part of her brain was the captain on a sinking ship, lost in the water booming through the cabin windows. "I'm sorry for that joke," she said, astounded at the words pouring out. "I'm so sorry, I love you, too, we can fix this, it'll be okay, you're an asshole but I think what we have is really good and we'll get through it, forget about that bitch…"

She reached for his hand and he took it. Wet palm to wet palm. Fingers knotted. Her knees shaking.

"Okay, okay," the nurse snapped. "If could all just *calm down* for a second, I need to explain something to you."

Alec squeezed her hand once before letting go. Wiping his nose with the back of his wrist, he said, "No blowtorch?"

"No," the nurse said. "But we're going to have to call the fire department. They have a diamond-tipped saw that can cut through titanium, and before you freak out again, they're very precise with it. I've seen them do it before."

"How many titanium cock-rings do you get in here?" Julia asked.

"Without breaking any kind of patient confidentiality rules, let's just say I've been forced to become an expert in every substance you can make a cock-ring from." The nurse gestured at the ring. "At least we're not amputating. That's always dramatic."

The hospital called the fire department. Fifteen minutes later, a group of firefighters appeared in the ER, dressed in their heavy jackets, carrying an absurd amount of gear. One of them hefted the ring saw, a terrifying piece of hardware with a two-stroke engine and a ten-inch blade—the kind of machinery you used to slice through a car door, not a tiny sex toy. Fortunately for everyone involved, Alec fainted at the sight of it.

"I love you, I love you, I love you, I love you," Julia whispered in his ear, still not quite understanding why she said it, as the saw roared and the ring popped free and Alec's penis ejected a celebratory spray of piss and blood.

The next month, they moved in together.

NINE

Kelby paused at the bottom of the steps, arms extended wide, twisting on his heels so they could admire his unmarked torso. He bent and pinched the torn edges of his jeans and pulled the holes wide so they could see his smooth legs.

"No," Alec said, struggling to his feet. "No, no, that's impossible."

"It's very possible," Kurt said, his unblinking gaze fixed on Kelby. "It's more possible than I ever believed."

But it was Moira who drew Julia's attention—Moira scrambling back until her spine touched the far wall. Moira like a cat frightened by an intruder, hackles raised, ready to fight to the death.

Julia decided to follow her example, backing to the doorway that led to the kitchen and the rooms beyond. If something truly terrible happened, she could barricade herself behind a few doors while she figured out what—

Wait, *if* something truly terrible happened?

Something terrible was already well underway.

How else to explain the formerly dead dude on the stairs, buzzing with superhuman vigor?

Hopefully he doesn't try to eat your brains!

Shut the hell up, she snapped back. Alec was right: it was impossible. Maybe Kelby had a twin hiding out in the dunes who slipped into the bunker while they were all downstairs and dressed in Kelby's bloody clothing before showing himself. No, that was ridiculous. Besides, if there was a twin, Moira would know about him, and she wouldn't freak out.

Maybe this was a mass hallucination. A secret ingredient in the food bars, courtesy of those Silicon Valley bros who loved experimenting with mushrooms and strange fungi. Maybe this bunker was part of an experiment to test hallucinatory psychedelics in a controlled environment, the better for the billionaire to profit off some key biomedical investments—

She slapped herself. Not too hard, but enough to snap her thoughts out of their downward spiral. The sound of her palm striking flesh was oddly loud, echoing off the concrete and sidewalk. Kelby turned to her.

"If you doubt," he said, "you're more than welcome to come over and touch. Feel my side. Feel my legs."

"How?" she asked, increasingly sure this wasn't a hallucination. It didn't feel like any of her drug trips from college, at least.

"The universe works in mysterious ways, I guess." Kelby shrugged, bouncing on the balls of his feet. "Just because you haven't seen something happen, doesn't mean it can't happen, agree?"

She had no answer to that. Weren't people supposed to go insane when they witnessed something beyond their comprehension? But she only felt a little confusion, as if confronted with a particularly vexing calculus problem. Maybe her brain was shielding itself, because if she went insane at this moment—dropped to her knees, drooling and gibbering—someone would hurt her.

"What if it violates physics?" Alec asked. "Or biology?" He sounded strong, normal, but his good leg shook wildly.

Julia tried signaling him with her eyes: keep your mouth shut. The last thing this situation needed was Alec the Expert trying to mansplain why something shouldn't exist.

"I don't see why anyone should pay attention to those things." Kelby laughed as if he'd never heard anything so ridiculous. "What you need to know is that I'm here and I'm hungry as a hog on crystal meth. What's this place got to eat?"

"Cheez Kneez," Kurt said vacantly. He shook his head, his eyes clearing. "And these weird energy bars. I'd stay away from the bars."

"Not in the mood for either of those things, anyway. I need serious protein." Kelby's gaze drifted across the courtyard before settling on the fish tank embedded into the wall. "And what have we here?"

"I don't know what kind they are," Julia said. "There might be more food in the kitchen?" The sight of a walking dead man hadn't snapped her mind, but her forehead prickled with sweat as a fresh rush of adrenaline zipped through her veins.

"Doubt it," Kelby said, walking over to the fish tank and pressing his hand against the cool glass. The fish gaped at the giant looming over them.

"They didn't do anything to you," Moira said, so quietly Julia almost missed it.

"That's not a factor in the equation," Kelby said. "It's never about who did what to whom. It's about who's hungry, and who's protein."

Julia shifted to Kurt, who stood with his back to Alec, the pistol dangling from his hand, his face suffused with the quiet peace of someone absorbed in a church service. If Alec could sneak over, he might have a chance of grabbing the gun, and then—

What? Even if they shot all three of these weirdo hikers in the face with these useless pepper bullets and evacuated the property at a good rate of speed despite Alec's damaged ass, they were stuck with the same list of problems as before. Julia grit her teeth.

Kelby's hand on the fish tank glass curled into a fist. "I had a lot of time to think just now," he said.

"It hasn't been that long," Kurt said. "You were… out… for a few minutes. It was the blood, wasn't it? The blood did something. We put a lot of it into you."

"Or maybe the universe just likes the cut of my jib." Kelby tapped his knuckles against the glass. "While I was deep in this nowhere void, just thinking, I got obsessed with this idea that humans evolved from apes, what, a couple hundred thousand years ago?"

"I thought you didn't believe in biology," Alec said, and flashed Julia a cheeky grin.

Julia drew a finger across her throat: shut up.

Kelby shrugged. "So, evolution brought us to our current point as a species, like, a long time ago. Like five hundred thousand years, maybe a million." Another fist-bump against the glass, a little harder this time. "We're walking around through the grassland or wherever, thinking like we do now, acting like we do now, making stupid jokes like we do now. Nothing ever ends, everything just keeps going round and round again. But we didn't start building cities and pyramids and governments and all the rest of that useless crap until, what, fifty thousand years ago?"

"Egyptian pyramids were built three thousand years ago," Alec said.

Kurt turned toward Alec, his hand flexing on the pistol's grip, his eyebrows raised.

The fish bobbed to Kelby's eye-level, ready to fight this intruder threatening their fortress. Kelby placed his knuckles against the tank and rotated his fist, as if trying to screw his arm through the glass. "Okay, whatever date we want to set here, the fact remains there's this huge gap of a couple hundred thousand years where people are walking around, people just like us, but they're not building what you might call 'civilization.' And if they're not doing that, what are they doing?"

"You're the guy with the theory," Moira said.

"I think they were just living their lives," Kelby continued. "In all that time, I'm positive people toyed with all kinds of ways of doing things—democracy, authoritarianism. They probably wandered where they wanted to wander, settled where they wanted to settle—"

"And had a life expectancy of thirty years, give or take," Alec said. "I'll take modern civilization any day."

"You think you'll live to see thirty?" Kelby's head rotated until his black eyes found Alec. The rest of his body stiff, his fist still squeaking and twisting on the glass.

"I hope so." Alec swallowed hard.

"Back then, maybe once you made it past childhood, your chances of living to a ripe old age suddenly shot up," Kelby said, focused again on the fish. "Like every other time in history, even today. These ancient people, they're wandering around, just living, being happy. They didn't build huge cities. They didn't invent all kinds of useless crap. They weren't locked to a desk and credit-card bills and expectations of what society wants."

"Ah, I get it," Kurt said, grinning.

Kelby studied Kurt's reflection in the glass. "Get what?"

"It's like the three of us. The holy trinity. We're out there, always moving, living by our wits." Kurt's grin wavered. "Right? We're not buying into anyone's program here."

Kelby's fist drew back and slammed into the tank, hard enough to shake the glass and send the fish scattering to the bottom. "No, no, you're just stating clichés," he said. "I'm not talking about the mission. I don't care about our stupid mission anymore. I want to live how we were always meant to live as a species, before someone decided we all needed to lock down, live our lives in these tight little patterns. Because you know where that's gotten us? Nowhere."

Kurt raised his hands, palms out. He was maybe fifty pounds heavier than Kelby, and yet from Julia's position he seemed so much smaller, a little kid trying to argue a point of logic with a parent. "Whatever you're feeling," Kurt said, "we're okay with that. You've had a long day."

"That wasn't a boar out there. You thought it was a boar, but it was something different," Kelby said. "When it sank its tusks into me, we had a moment, an incredible moment. It had things to teach me."

Moira moaned.

"Moira," Kelby said. "Do you like your life?"

Moira nodded vigorously.

"You're wrong. Nobody likes their life all the time." Kelby punched the fish tank again, as hard as before. Boom. The fish circling in panic. "And I bet our ancestors a million years ago liked their lives even less. But they were free."

"I don't get this," Kurt said. "Can you help me out? I don't understand."

"That's okay. I'll make you." Kelby's reflected gaze on Julia, freezing her every cell. "I'll make all of you."

The sun must have shifted overhead, because the glow filtering through the skylight brightened, intensifying into a spotlight on Kelby. His jawline blazed through the thin forest of his beard, his eyeballs flaring into pocket galaxies, the irises like swirls of glowing dust a million light-years across. Julia thinking again of kings' ancient tombs deep in the earth, skulls crusted with diamonds and rubies, the bone etched with symbols of immense power. Except none of that was the oddest thing, the one detail she'd somehow missed in the blood and chaos of the past hour.

No, the oddest thing was how much Kelby looked like Alec. They practically shared a jawline and chin, the same slope of the forehead and the shape of the eyes. They could have been brothers. Except Alec was an only child, with no cousins she could remember. Maybe this was a freakish coincidence, or a trick of the light.

Kelby balled his fist again and, twisting his hips, punched the fish tank one more time. A pop, and a hairline crack appeared in the glass. Water seeped down the concrete wall. Another pop, another crack running perpendicular to the first, and the glass gave way, followed by a small flood.

Moira and Kurt retreated as the water splashed over their ankles on its way to the small drain in the center of the courtyard. The architects had designed the floor to slope slightly, like an enormous sink, so Julia and Alec stayed dry in their spots by the walls.

Kelby extended his arm through the jagged hole in the glass, careful to avoid the edges. The fish swirled in the tank's last three inches of silty water. He paused to study them before his hand darted down. A thrashing, foamy spray, a spiny fish between his thumb and forefinger.

Julia wondered if the fish was poisonous. A reclusive billionaire who owned a luxury doomsday bunker might stock it with a deadly species, because in the face of starvation or radiation sickness you might prefer a quicker way out, one little stab with a toxic spine and you were off to eternity.

"Protein," Kelby said, and swallowed the fish. Chewed, the crunch of tiny bones loud over the gurgle of water and Moira's rapid breathing. And swallowed, his attention on Julia as he did so.

TEN

A speaker clicked overhead.

"You have damaged valuable property," the recruiter said, every syllable snappy-sharp as a switchblade. It was a tone that promised endless lawsuits and trumped-up charges and whatever else a billionaire could throw at one of the peasants.

"What?" Kelby reached into his mouth with two fingers, digging around. "The fish?" He drew a thin bone from between his lips and held it overhead for the cameras' inspection. "I wouldn't say 'valuable.' It was tasteless. Just like this place's design."

Based on how Kelby was still upright, Julia guessed the fish wasn't poisonous, either. Too bad.

"What do you want?" the recruiter asked.

"The same thing we wanted in Siberia, and Kuril, and New Zealand, and here," Kurt said, almost shouting as he stepped into the center of the courtyard. "You can't negotiate with us. We know what you're up to, and we're going to stop it."

"Maybe we should just leave," Moira whispered.

"No," Kurt shouted, pointing a thick finger at her. "We're so close to finishing this. One more site after this, maybe two, then California…"

The recruiter chuckled. *"Just one site? Maybe two? Oh, you poor, delusional… hippies."*

Kelby swallowed the bone. "Your boss represents everything wrong with deep history. He's built his fortune on top of activities that prevent the human race from just wandering through endless territory, being happy, playing with different modes of government the same way a child might try on different hats. On top of that …"

"Hey, Kelby, we're getting a little off-track here," Kurt said.

"Shut your mouth." Kelby bared his teeth. "You're not innocent here. You've forgotten man's fundamental purpose, too."

Kurt waved the gun. "Let's all stay very calm here, okay? I'm the leader of our happy little band, remember?"

"There are no leaders in utopia," Kelby said, taking a step toward him.

"You better leave," Julia told them. "They have a reserve team nearby. It's, like, a SWAT team or something. They'll kill you."

"I'm beyond life and death," Kelby said, taking another step toward Kurt.

"Not if they shoot you with a grenade launcher or something," Alec offered. "It's hard to come back from the dead when you're in little pieces splattered all over the ceiling."

Alec saying 'little pieces' made Julia think of cutting things up made her think—holy crap—of the chainsaw in the maintenance room only a few feet away. She knew the keycode. If she and Alec could get inside, they could wait these fuckers out until help arrived. And if any of them tried to break in, she could slice off an arm or two.

Moira laughed and shook her head. "It's not going to happen."

"What isn't happening?" Julia asked, startled. It was almost as if this weird woman had read her thoughts. *Could* she read her thoughts?

"The rescue team," Moira said. "They told you a rescue team is coming? That help is on the way? It doesn't exist. They just tell you that to keep you calm."

"Calm? Why?" Julia said, noticing for the first time how, with everyone's attention focused elsewhere, Alec had stepped closer to Kurt, no more than five feet behind the big weirdo. Was he going for the gun?

"There's a drone coming," Kurt said, keeping the pistol fixed on Kelby. "Much bigger than the one they keep here for surveillance. It's loaded with missiles. Any of these facilities are compromised, they fly the drone in and blow it up. Bury everyone and everything in rubble."

"By facilities, you mean bunkers." Julia tried to keep her gaze on anything but Alec, who had restarted his slow creep toward Kurt, using the bigger man's bulk to shield his movements from Kelby and Moira.

Moira sighed and shook her head. "Oh, you sweet but deluded child. You don't have the first clue, do you?"

"I wouldn't be so hard on her. She's learning," Kelby said, and turned his face to the ceiling. "You mind if I tell her?"

An electronic hiss like a drawn-out sigh. *"It doesn't matter now,"* the recruiter said.

"Not yet," Kurt said. "We don't know if—"

Alec leapt for the gun. Maybe he'd envisioned it beforehand as an elegant snatch, the kind of thing Jason Statham or Jet Li pulled off in the action movies he loved, but his mangled ass turned it into a shambling lurch, his upper body colliding with Kurt's ribs as his hand slapped the pistol's barrel.

Kurt's finger squeezed reflexively on the trigger. The pistol boomed, slamming Julia's eardrums as she stood, ready to back Alec's play.

Kelby's head snapped back and the air around him flared red.

Julia was across the space, her hand on Kurt's wrist, helping Alec bend the man's arm toward the floor. Up close, Kurt stank of dirt and blood and snack food, and she might have found that nauseating if the stench of pepper spray hadn't overwhelmed her in the next instant. Her nose stinging again, her tear-ducts squirting like fountains. Alec's breath loud in her ear, his thin forearm wrapping around Kurt's throat.

Kurt drew back, and she shifted her grip from his wrist to the pistol, the metal hot. If she could get the weapon away from him, she would shoot Moira and Kelby, just for funsies, and drag Alec's semi-useless ass up the stairs. Every instinct told her to head for the maintenance room but what had Kurt said about a motherfucking drone with *missiles*?

True or not, staying in the bunker was the worst possible idea. They'd take their chances outside, in the open air.

Her nose jetted snot, her throat tight, but she knew these crazy pepper-spray bullets wouldn't kill her, and the effect didn't last long. Yanking the pistol away, she reached her other hand past Kurt's heaving bulk, gripping Alec's shoulder. A planet-sized weight crashed into her jaw, and the world went s—

ELEVEN

One of Alec's scuzzier crypto-bro friends conned a few Silicon Valley venture capitalists out of fifty million dollars, promising to build them an app that would allow people to convert their paychecks to the cryptocurrency of their choice: Bitcoin, Ethereum, Litecoin, Dogecoin, MatrixCoin, ZenBucks, and so much more. *I'm not jealous,* Alec insisted as he sketched out the logos of imaginary companies in a notebook. *I'll beat him one day.*

The friend invited them to a party to celebrate his newfound money spigot. The venue was a rooftop bar with artificial palm trees wrapped in purple neon. The effect was supposed to be cheerfully kitsch, but Julia just thought the alien lighting made everyone look like shit, even the models their host hired to prettify the crowd. The entertainment was a rapper whose biggest hit had climbed the charts three decades ago.

"I want to go home," Julia told Alec after an hour. A headache throbbed behind her left eye, intensifying whenever one of Alec's friends mentioned tokens or decentralized applications or the blockchain.

"I know," Alec said, rubbing her back. "But we have to stay, okay? If I want my business to succeed, I need to make connections."

"You don't have a business," she said, wagging her empty glass at the bartender for a refill. Maybe alcohol would help murder the pain in her head. "Not yet."

"Don't say that," he said. His hand dropped from her back. "Don't you dare."

"But it's true, isn't it? Baby, I'm sorry, but it's true. We have jobs. *Good* jobs, especially given the shit economy we just graduated into. But we're not starting any companies." She'd accidentally skewered his ego, sure, but he was delusional about this.

"I have the company in my head," he said. "The rest is easy. You know what the problem is? You don't believe in me."

This is escalating quickly, she thought. "No, I do. Look, how about you stay, and I'll grab an Uber."

"No."

"Excuse me?"

"I need you here." His hand on her waist, pulling her close. His fingertips pressing hard into her skin. "Too many incels here. People need to see I'm with someone."

He was sweet to her most of the time. That was the worst thing about these blowups. She gripped his wrist and pried his hand away. "No," she said. "No, I'm going."

She expected him to put up more of a fight, but he leaned back and took a sip of his drink and offered her a kicked-puppy look. Sometimes his green eyes brimming with sadness could change her mind, but not tonight. She gave him a dry peck on the cheek and swam through the crowd for the elevators.

On the way down to the lobby, her phone buzzed. She pulled it out of her purse, the lock screen bright with texts—not from Alec, as she expected, but her brother Freddie, who lived a few blocks away, on the edge of downtown. The texts themselves were gibberish, long streams of emojis and nonsense words, which was a sign that Freddie was high again. Shit. What other horrors would this evening offer?

She decided to walk. It would help clear her head. Freddie was waiting for her on the steps of his rundown apartment building, a cigarette with a long ash plugged into the corner of his mouth, a ratty pigeon perched on his left shoulder. Before she could ask whether the pigeon was stuffed— Freddie had a habit of buying odd things from pawn shops, often using them as props in one of his increasingly unfunny con games—it flapped down to his wrist and pecked some breadcrumbs from Freddie's cupped right hand.

"I'm having one of those nights," she said. "What's up?"

"I got a new friend," Freddie said, slurring the words.

"I can see that. That's why you're texting me? Are you safe?"

"Better friend than you." Freddie stood, waving his arm. The pigeon flew off. "Where's my cash, sis?"

"I don't owe you any cash," she said, glancing up and down the sidewalk. Nobody in sight on this grimy little street. Not good. Over the past few years, as her brother had drifted in and out of rehab, her love for him had shifted. She wanted the best for him, but after he shoved her one afternoon, she also feared what he could do while the beast was riding him.

"You're dressed nice," he said, and shook his head. "No money? Yeah, right."

"Came from a party."

"With your twat boyfriend?" He approached her with a gangly dance, his arms raised, a smirk slicing his face.

"He's not a twat," she said, her cheeks flushing.

"Oh, he is. He called me a twat, but he's the twat." That smirk hardening into something worse. "I texted him, too. He told me to fuck off."

"Well, I'm not responsible for what Alec does," she said, straightening her spine. It was just like dealing with a bear: if you showed fear, you died.

"Look, just give me the cash you owe me," he said, his dance turning into a leap, snatching her elbow before she could step back. He smelled like smoke. When they were kids, they would sneak a few cigarettes from their parents' packs and sit on the roof and smoke while talking about all the places they wanted to see, Kyoto and Prague and Paris—especially Paris. Useless dreams, the kind you tried to forget when you woke up in your tiny bedroom with its cracking walls and worn furniture.

"Let go of me," she said, trying to pull away, but he tightened his grip and she thought: this is it. This is where my lovely brother finally hurts me, not because he wants to, but because of this monkey on his back. This is—

A blur, a split-second sense of incredible mass heaving through space, and Alec appeared out of nowhere, crashing into Freddie. The impact sent Julia stumbling back on her impractical shoes, losing her balance so she crashed onto the sidewalk on her ass. Freddie, meanwhile, hit the scrubby lawn, his eyes fluttering closed.

Alec's hand slid around her wrist, helping her upright. "I'm so sorry," he told her, kissing her face, her neck, her lips. "I'm so sorry for what I said before, and when Freddie started texting me I was so worried, so I came here and…"

"It's okay," she told him, breaking from his embrace so she could kneel next to Freddie. Her brother was still breathing, but if he'd taken something dangerous the hospital would need to flush his system. She pulled out her phone, ready to dial 911.

"I don't care about a stupid company," Alec said, babbling faster, probably from the adrenaline still burning through his blood. "I'll do whatever you want. Let's get married, okay? How do you feel about that? I think that's a great idea. We should do it."

She had the phone to her ear, 911 already putting her on hold. "Can we talk about literally anything else right now?"

TWELVE

Kelby knelt, scooped a handful of fish-tank water from the courtyard floor, and splashed it in his eyes.

"What do you know about skull-fucking?" he asked Julia, relaxed and friendly, like he wanted her opinion on peanut butter or whether the Giants had a chance of winning the Super Bowl this season.

"What?" Julia croaked. She lay on the floor, against a section of courtyard wall without a built-in bench, her upper body sprawled across Alec's legs. Two shots of pepper spray in under an hour left her eyes aching and her vision watery. Her arms twisted behind her back, her wrists tied together with what felt like rough twine—her shoulders and elbows already tingling from the unnatural position.

"Skull-fucking," Kelby said, standing, thrusting his hips.

Wherever this was going, it was nowhere good. She twisted at the waist for a better view of Alec, who was out cold, his reddened face crusted with tears and drying snot. His hands trapped beneath his body, no doubt tied like hers.

"Look," Kurt said. "Can we talk about this?" He knelt in the center of the courtyard, his hands bound behind his back with brightly colored twine. Moira lying on her side beside him, her wrists and ankles hog-tied in front of her. The pistol was nowhere in sight.

"No, no, we can't." Kelby walked over to him. "I've been sick of your shit for a long time. Since Siberia, at least. So focused on this 'mission,' even though you know it won't do jack squat for the world in the end. It's just your ego, thinking you can stick it to the man."

"We've had our problems," Kurt babbled. "I acknowledge that. I pulled us too far, too fast. Maybe didn't discuss our priorities in enough detail. But you know what's happening here is an abomination and needs to be stopped, right? We can't change the world, but we can do—"

"Hush," Kelby told him. He shrugged off his blood-smeared raincoat and the shredded shirt beneath. His lean torso pale as alabaster, rippling with muscles. Next, he unbuckled his pants and let them drop around his ankles, revealing a dirty pair of boxer-briefs. The underwear fabric twitched.

Oh shit, Julia thought. *He's getting a stiffy.*

"Little lady," Kelby said, talking to Julia even as he held Kurt's gaze. "I asked you a question before. Better answer me."

"I don't know anything about that," Julia said. "Why would I know anything about sick shit like that?"

That was a lie. Kelby didn't know it, but Julia was one of relatively few people on this bright blue orb who knew a little something about consensual skull-fucking. One of Julia's former co-workers at a bar named the Blue Spot, a goth princess named Roberta, had lost her left eye in a childhood accident with a sharp stick. And one night after closing, once they'd downed too many shots of vodka, Roberta had confessed her boyfriend loved it when she popped out her glass eyeball and let him shove the tip of what she called his "throbbing member" into the socket.

He can't fit the whole head in, Roberta confided, giggling. *He just sort of moves it back and forth a little bit. Doesn't take much.*

You let him nut in there? Julia asked, both repulsed and oddly intrigued.

Roberta shook her head. *Fuck no. What if it leaked somewhere in there? I might never speak in complete sentences again.*

Julia had never told anyone that story, and why would she start now? It wouldn't help her out of this. As she lay there, watching Kelby watch Kurt like prey, she tried pulling her wrists apart. Kelby had given her a half-inch of slack. She wiggled her forearms, trying to be subtle about it, hoping it would loosen the knot a little.

"Well, we're about to conduct a little demonstration," Kelby said.

"*Please*," Kurt wheezed. "I know we had our differences, but you used to be such a nice kid, you believed in this, you remember, you believed in this, we had such good times out on the road and you're not the same person, are you, you're not the same person you're not the same person you're…"

"Hush." Kelby pushed his boxer-briefs to his knees, shook them down to his ankles. He was fully erect, his cock on the larger side and webbed with veins like the tributaries of a dark river. "You're not understanding. But you will, don't you fret. I'm going to insert that knowledge in you."

Kurt whined between his teeth and squeezed his eyes shut as Kelby placed his palms on either side of the man's head. Kelby's penis bobbing like a dowsing rod an inch from Kurt's nose. Kelby's fingers tightened, digging into Kurt's smooth skin.

On the floor, Moira twitched. "Please, Kelby, you don't have to do this..."

"Hush," Kelby said, bending his twists. The tendons in Kurt's neck strained like cables as he tried to keep his head level, but Kelby was too strong. Inch by painful inch, Kurt's head dipped until the throbbing purple tip of Kelby's penis brushed his closed left eye.

Julia wanted to look away, but her every muscle felt cold and immobile as ice. Frozen in place not just by the horrific spectacle, but also the overwhelming sense that Kelby, beneath his beard and hiker-grime, looked almost exactly like Alec. What had Kurt said about blood? *We put a lot of it into you.* Had Alec's blood somehow brought Kelby back from the dead? Even worse, was it transforming Kelby into some kind of... Alec clone?

Sure. Why not? Anything was possible today, right? Insane laughter threatened to boil up her throat, and she inhaled to tamp it down, Buddha breathing, smoothing blue deep into her lungs. Breathe, breathe, breathe. Don't lose your shit.

With one hand gripping the base of his cock, the other on the back of Kurt's skull, Kelby thrust himself forward. His cockhead jammed against Kurt's eye socket. Kurt yelped. Unlike Julia's old colleague and her boyfriend, the parts weren't quite syncing up here; the tip pushed against the eyeball maybe a quarter of an inch before thudding against the bone.

"Hold still," Kelby said, bouncing on his toes, tightening his grip on Kurt's skull, and thrust forward, harder. Kurt's moan rose to a wheezy shriek, punctuated by a soft popping.

Kelby's flexing ass-cheeks hid the worst of it from Julia's view, but she could hear a faint squeaking as he thrust rapidly into the new opening. Kelby breathing harder and harder.

"Julia?" Alec whispered, barely louder than breath.

Not daring to say anything, Julia squeezed Alec's knee twice.

"I love you," Alec whispered. "I love you so much."

"I love you, too," she murmured. "Always have. Always will."

A click from the wall beside her, more felt than heard. A cool rectangle of concrete pressing against her shoulder. She angled her head slightly. Another drawer had appeared, like the one that held the pistol and the non-lethal rounds.

Kelby thrusting longer strokes, rocking on the very tips of his toes. Moira crying softly, not loud enough to drown out the *slurp-squish*. Julia figured Kurt was dead by this point, because how much abuse could a brain take? Its front parts contained the powers of words and reasoning, she remembered from high school biology, and just an inch or two beyond that were all the sections you needed to keep breathing, moving, loving, living.

A guttural moan. Did Kelby make that sound? Was this almost over? No, it was Kurt, his mouth flapping open and slapping shut, spraying saliva, opening again, speech boiling out: "All discourse is algorithmic. My belief in God is totally fluid."

"Fluid, yeah," Kelby muttered through gritted teeth. "Hold still, buddy."

"Everyone has an authoritarian impulse, and that's okay," Kurt told him, warbling in pitch as his brain's language centers turned to jelly. "You just need to question that narrative."

Slurp-squish.

"The narrative."

Slurp-squish.

"The narrative."

Moving as slowly as she dared, Julia shoved closer to the wall, trying to ignore Alec's gasp of pain as she pressed her weight on his bad side. She scrabbled her fingers behind her, feeling the edge of the drawer. It opened to her gentle pressure, the lid scraping against her forearm. She felt cold foam, pebbled plastic, a metal cylinder. Another gun? Was there a whole arsenal embedded in the courtyard walls?

"Question the narrative?" Kelby screeched, drawing back on his heels, his ass tightening. "You didn't question a *single fucking thing*—"

With that, he thrust forward, hopping onto one foot, as his hands slammed Kurt's head onto his crotch. Screaming as he did so. The thick splatter of something unmentionable hitting the floor between his straining feet.

Julia wrapped three fingers around the metal tube and pulled forward, and yes, it was a gun in her hands, a revolver just like the other one. Hopefully loaded with real bullets. But the gun was useless so long as her hands were tied behind her back.

Alec's eyes on her, wide and frantic.

Maybe she could slip her tethered hands over her legs and feet, a bit of old-fashioned contortionism. She was flexible enough, right? She did yoga for years. Well, for a year. No, more like six months, but it was a hard class run by a crazy Israeli dude, and by the end of it she could do that move where you downward-dogged on one leg while sticking the other one in the air.

She slid off Alec's legs onto the cold floor, making sure she landed on her ass. Breathe in blue, exhale green. Blue, green, blue, green. You can do this. She set the heavy revolver on the concrete—no sense in blowing a hole in her backside by accident—and scooted a few inches to the right, then sat on her hands. Paused to check on the horrific scene in the center of the courtyard.

Kelby faced away from her, his ass still pumping hard. A low hum that Julia thought was coming from inside the walls until she realized it was issuing from Kelby himself. Like a machine trying to reboot.

So far, so good. Lifting up, she moved her tethered hands past her hips and thighs, toward her knees. Bending forward as she did so. Fresh ache in her lower back as she stretched. Her stomach fat piling against the band of her underwear.

Moira tilted her head toward Julia.

A jolt of fear up Julia's spine, freezing her in place.

Moira offered an almost imperceptible nod.

Julia, returning the nod, began to move again. Hunched as far forward as she could, her hands almost to her ankles. She bent her knees, trying to bring her ankles closer to her hands, but her elbows jammed against her kneecaps.

The first twinge of panic. No, calm down. Stay flexible. Blue, green, blue, green, blue. She tried shifting her knees and elbows so all her parts slid smoothly past each other, but her wrists were tied together too tightly, making it impossible to raise her elbows high, she was jammed in this stupid pseudo-yoga position, call it the Dead Girl Pose, ready for the slaughter—

"What are you doing?" Kelby asked.

Kelby's head turning like an owl, his body still facing forward with Kurt's head impaled on his crotch.

Alec coughed, croaked, "You're a sick fuck. Look at me, you sick fuck."

He was trying his best to distract, but Kelby was locked on the gun, on her, reading her intention clear as a book. His eyebrows rose, his teeth gritting, as he gripped Kurt's shoulders and tried to pull out. With a moist squeak, his penis slid maybe two inches from Kurt's skull—and stuck. Kelby's hips bucked, frantic, and his fingernails dug into Kurt's pale scalp, ripping the skin bloody, but neither move popped him loose.

The lunatic part of Julia's mind pictured Kurt's skull from the inside, Kelby's blood-bulging cockhead jammed against the inside of the eye-socket like a thumb in a Chinese finger-trap.

"Don't you fucking dare," Kelby said, yanking harder.

Julia drew back and dipped forward again, harder, hoping she needed just a bit of momentum to pop her elbows over the impossible mountains of her knees, but bone clashed against bone and she was stuck, fuck, what now? Alec also scrambling for the gun, wincing in pain, too slow, useless.

Screeching, every muscle in his back red and flexing, Kelby twisted Kurt's head like a carpenter working loose a jammed screw, and his cock popped loose with a splash of blood and fluid. Kelby spun on Julia and Alec, his waist coated gelatinous red. His hands locked into dripping claws.

Kurt's body slid to the floor, his last breath whispering between blood-flecked lips, the eye-hole oozing. The raincoat barely yellow anymore.

Kelby marched for Julia, his screech hardening into words loud enough to shatter concrete, as loud as the bunker's speakers:

"You'll understand—
"

Julia's brain short-circuited, no brilliant ideas left, no deep blue inhales, just the idiot squawk of nerve endings too exhausted to fight or flight, and—

Moira on the floor yelling something, waving her hands tied in front of her—

The inner gremlin that had badgered Julia the whole day, the one that sometimes sounded like the recruiter and sometimes like Alec and sometimes like her brother, the one she hated, was still alive at the base of her brain, still giving orders aboard the sinking ship, and it said *throw her that gun you useless bitch or you're going to die*—

And Julia's tired nerves obeyed. Powered her forearm to sweep the pistol in front of her feet, powered her feet to lash out, spinning the weapon across the wet floor toward Moira's grasping fingers—

Kelby sidestepped, trying to catch the pistol as it passed, and missed. Moira had the pistol in her tied hands, thumbing back the hammer, barrel up—

"*Lethal force* definitely *authorized*," the recruiter said.

Kelby rolled his eyes to the ceiling. "You're a useless shadow on the wall, you dumb—"

Moira aimed, adjusted, pulled the trigger. Boom. Kelby folded on himself, clutching his stomach. Moira fired again and again and again and again, the explosion of ammunition accompanied by the sledgehammer thump of lead into hard flesh. Julia, raised on a lifetime of action movies, thought five heavy-caliber bullets to the torso would produce a lot of gory spray, but Kelby seemed to absorb them without a spilled drop of blood as he fell on his face in the pinkish water.

THIRTEEN

After the fire department sawed the titanium cock-ring off Alec, Julia had shared a cigarette with the nurse on the hospital loading docks. *Man,* Julia said, sucking down half the cancer-stick in a single pull. *How do you deal with it?*

The nurse breathed in smoke, blasted it out her nose. *Deal with what?*

The intensity of it.

The nurse shrugged. *The human brain is an amazing thing. You can get used to anything. Literally anything. Even the worst things.*

Julia fixed on that idea as she scrambled across the wet courtyard, swinging wide of Kelby's body. When she reached the fish tank, she stood, twisted around, and, as carefully as she could, felt for the jagged hole. Raised her arms high and slotted the rope around her wrists against a sharp glass edge. Moving her wrists up and down, she sawed off the rope.

Once her hands were free, she retrieved a knife from the kitchen and freed Moira and Alec. She had faced down an invasion climaxing with a vicious skull-fucking and yet she felt remarkably fine, at least if you defined 'fine' as a little shaky in the knees and slightly nauseous but otherwise upright and moving right along. Maybe it was all the adrenaline and she would really feel it later, like how soldiers developed PTSD once they returned from the battlefield.

She wished the nurse was here. The nurse would know.

Moira stood, rubbing her chafed wrists. Before slicing away the rope, Julia had taken the pistol and popped open the cylinder, verifying a single live round left before slapping it closed and slipping the weapon into her pocket. Moira had saved their lives and helped free Julia, sure, but Julia still had a lot of questions about all this weird bullshit.

"Thank you," Moira said.

"No, thank you," Julia said, slipping her hands beneath Alec's armpits as he levered himself off the floor. His face still puffy from the pepper spray, the left side of his jaw purpling from either a punch or hitting the concrete. She kissed him lightly on the temple.

Moira crab-walked to Kurt and ran her fingers lightly across the crusted cheek, the cored-out eye. She murmured something Julia didn't quite catch.

"You got the gun?" Alec said, leaning his weight on her. "Shoot that prick again. Make sure it's done."

"No, it's over," Julia said. "See?"

Kelby lay curled on the floor to their left, five perfect holes in his chest and stomach. There was a curious lack of blood, but maybe that's what happened when a storm of bullets ended your life in the half-second between heartbeats. Something about his pose reminded Julia of a saint in an Italian Renaissance painting, prostrate before God and the angels. She still thought he resembled Alec's long-lost twin.

"Good enough," Alec said. He was solid on his feet but kept his arms around Julia, his heart fluttering against her shoulder. "What now?"

Moira stood and wiped her nose with the back of her hand. "I'm sorry this happened."

"Why did this happen?" Julia asked. "You said there was some kind of mission?"

"That's right." Stripping off her bloody raincoat, Moira draped it over Kurt's wrecked face. Her underlayer was a faded nylon windbreaker and a pair of black cargo pants saturated with dirt. "But it doesn't matter now. I guess it's over."

"Tell us," Alec said. "You owe us that much."

"It's probably easier if I show you," Moira said. "There's a place outside with solar panels and stuff like that? It has a shed, or a building of some kind?"

Julia nodded. "Yeah. It's on top of the hill."

"Okay," Moira said. "Let's go take a look. I don't know how much time we have."

"Because of the drone?" Alec said.

The speaker clicked. *"There is no drone coming to kill you,"* the recruiter said. *"You're to stay in place. Your paycheck depends on it."*

"You can take this job and shove it," Julia announced. "We're going home."

"Come on," Moira said, thudding toward the steps. "There's no time. No time."

"Stay," the recruiter said. *"Please."*

"No," Alec said. "You didn't give us the real gun until it was almost too late."

"We had no choice. We had to see."

"See what?" Alec snorted. "Some dude get a dick jammed in his skull? You get off on that?"

The nearest monitor flashed to life, displaying a video clip of Julia on the floor, tangled atop Alec. Judging by the angle, it had been recorded by the camera in the courtyard's far corner, which zoomed into her face as she said, *"I love you, too. Always have. Always will."*

"I still don't get it," Alec said.

Silence from the speakers.

"I'll tell you," Moira called to them from halfway up the steps. "Let's go. There's no time, no time, no time."

FOURTEEN

At the top of the steps, Julia spotted a few drops of blood on the concrete. Midway down the hallway, the drops became a thickening smear, a messy arrow swooping toward the front rooms. Red handprints on the walls, at waist-level but descending toward the floor. Signs of Kelby's resurrection in reverse, if his bleeding slackened as he rose.

In the front room where they'd tried to save Kelby's life, Moira kicked aside the discarded medical wrappers and the first aid kit, then sank to her knees and stuck a hand beneath the couch. Pulled out Kurt's blue backpack. "When you see what's inside here," she said, "you'll know. You'll believe."

"Oh, I believe," Alec said, grabbing his cane from the floor and giving it a jaunty twirl. "You could tell me anything at this point and I'd believe it. Aliens, whatever."

"Let's do it outside," Moira said, slipping past him through the doorway.

"Wait," Julia held up her hands. "Aren't we safer in here? I mean, this place is solid concrete, it was built to withstand missiles, right? We're out in the open, that drone will just splatter us."

"If I told you I've been in this building before, same layout and everything, and the drone brought it down, would you believe me?" Moira pointed at the ceiling. "Because you better believe me. There's safety outside, in the hills above the beach, the scrub, whatever. More places to hide in a wilderness than you think."

"Sure," Julia said.

They followed Moira down the hallway to the front door. The sun dipped toward a purpling horizon, the ocean darkening. In the distance, the frothy white line of the reef, its angles of coral like the bones of giants left there soon after the birth of the world. Julia paused at the top of the steps to suck down fresh air until her lungs strained, imagining it the purest blue, filling her with life.

She would never forget what happened inside. How could you? But holding that blessed air in her lungs, she believed everything might be okay in the end, for all of them.

"You want to show me the pathway to that shed?" Moira asked.

"Down the steps," Julia said. "Then around to the left, up that dune. It's a little trail that goes up the side of the hill here, between the rocks."

"Why don't we just run?" Alec said. "Get the fuck away from here?"

Moira sighed and unzipped the backpack, turned it upside-down so its contents spilled across the steps: energy bars and a water bottle and spare underwear and a strip of condoms and an old smartphone. She awakened the phone and tapped the Photos app, tilting the screen so they could see as she swiped through image after image.

Every image featured Alec and Julia somewhere in the bunker. Julia always in her peasant dress, Alec in some combination of t-shirt and jeans. In some of the shots, Alec held his cane. They were eating, laughing, watching television. Kurt and Kelby and Moira appeared in some of the shots, grinning or eating or holding up a weird piece of art for the camera's inspection.

"I don't remember any of this," Alec said.

"Because it didn't happen to you," Moira said, flicking the phone off and pocketing it. Marching down the stairs, she called over her shoulder, "Those were taken at the other facilities."

"Bullshit," Alec said. "It's a deepfake or something."

"It's not," Moira shot back. "And I can prove it. Come on."

They followed her down the steps and across the sand, Moira pausing for them to catch up before veering onto the path that ascended the side of the hill. "Okay, pop quiz," Moira said as they began to climb. "What's the name of the billionaire who owns this creepy little place?"

"That's easy, it's..." Julia trailed off. She had seen the billionaire's name hundreds, maybe thousands of times—you couldn't open the newsfeed on your phone without reading his latest gonzo statement about cryptocurrency or space flight or apps—and yet it eluded her in the moment, slipping beyond the border of memory. She balled her right hand and slammed it into her hip. Why couldn't she remember?

"It's okay," Moira said. "The billionaire's name is Alec."

"Like me?" Alec called out from behind Julia.

"He is you. Just much older." Moira paused, regarding them from her higher elevation.

Julia laughed. The bright sun needled her forehead, sweat trickling down her ribs. It was too hot out here, her blood buzzing against the inside of her skull—she must have misheard Moira. "What?"

"They're the same. Alec—the billionaire— built a bunch of facilities around the world," Moira shrugged, as if to say: *Rich assholes, what can you do?* "They're all similar to this one. Lots of concrete and gadgets in the middle of nowhere. They're not bunkers, though. They're... I guess you'd call them study facilities."

"Studying what?" Alec said, so wearily that Julia turned to him, concerned. Alec slumped over his cane, his shirt dark with sweat, the ocean a stark blue line behind him. It would have made for a great photograph under different circumstances.

"Studying you and Alec," Moira said. "We've found one of you and Alec in every facility. You're always wearing that dress. He's always got a bunch of shrapnel in him 'from Kyiv.'" She made air quotes. "By the way, that conflict ended a couple of decades ago—it didn't go well for Russia."

"What *the fuck*," Alec wheezed, bending further, seemingly ready to topple over.

Julia felt sick again. Her pulse fluttering against her temples, her armpits slick. "You mean like clones? Clones of us?"

"Yes. And however you're... created... there's something about your blood. We put it in Kelby, dear Kelby," Moira swallowed and wiped her eye with the back of her hand. "Sweet boy. Dumb as a rock—he really believed the moon landings were fake—but sweet. Whatever was down there wasn't him. Putting your blood in him, it changed him somehow."

It made him look a lot like Alec, Julia almost said. Had it given Kelby a big dose of Alec's intensity, as well? Is that why Kelby went berserk? Except Alec wasn't violent like that, even if he was given to crazed theories that explained life, the universe, and everything.

"I don't believe this," Alec said. "Clones? That's, like, twenty or thirty years away, in terms of technology. If it ever happens."

"Exactly," Moira said. "It did happen. Ten years ago, or thereabouts. Let me tell you, once the cost of cloning someone went down, porn got really weird."

A fresh breeze rasped over the sand. To their right, almost at the hill's crest, the bone-white circle of the skylight poked from its lava-rock socket like a dead eye. Julia scanned the sky for anything that looked like an incoming drone, loaded with missiles to splatter them all. Once the bunker was out of sight, it was such a beautiful landscape, the breakers pounding at the broad swaths of sand, the shoreline ridges rising into the hills. A world of solid things, far removed from all human concerns. She could sit down right here and let this world sweep over her, sink her into the dunes, safely beyond all the noise and lies and fury.

"Let's go," Moira said, waving a hand for them to follow as she crested the hill. When they arrived at the fence-lined enclosure, she turned to Julia. "You're going to have to shoot that lock off."

Julia touched the pistol poking from her pocket. "Why?"

Moira winked and tapped her temple. "What, you're saving that bullet for something? Because we both know you won't shoot me."

Aw, what the hell. Julia drew the weapon and aimed it at the lock. Squinted as she lined up the sights with the keyhole. Solid things. Focusing on this would push aside the insanity of clones and blood—if only for a moment.

She pulled the trigger. The lock blasted apart in a spray of sparks and metal. Moira stepped forward and kicked the gate open, marching into the enclosure without looking back. Julia was about to follow when Alec took her elbow with cold, shaking fingers.

She shrugged from his grasp and turned to him, placing her hand in his. He opened his mouth, but nothing came out. Speechless for once in his life. Under different circumstances, she might have made a joke about it, but his expression reminded her too much of the spiny fish trapped in the fish tank.

Letting his hand drop, she followed Moira into the enclosure. The woman had disappeared behind the hut containing the bunker's water filtration system and electronics, and when Julia took the corner, she found herself in an area shaded by scrubby brush. A narrow, rocky trail wound down the far slope.

"Where are you going?" Julia called, as the top of Moira's head dipped below the rise.

"Come on," Moira called back. "I don't think it's far."

"Gonna break my ankle," Alec muttered behind them.

Julia followed Moira down the path, digging her feet into the loose sand and rock. Every step kicked off a small avalanche. As they descended the hill, the brush fell away, revealing a narrow cove hemmed on its far side by black cliffs, its beaches bone-pale and immaculate. It was maybe two hundred yards up the coast from the bunker's front door, yet she had never ventured in this direction, and she wondered whether the billionaire had programmed her subconscious to avoid this spot—

You don't believe this clone shit, do you?

Except she did. She really did.

The ground leveled out. They stood at the cove's edge, ten yards from the breakers rumbling like artillery, the air thick with spray. It was thick with insects, too, swirling around their heads, nipping at their necks. Julia smelled the sour-sweet of rot, like a bucket of compost left too long in the sun.

Moira pointed at darker shapes poking from the wet sand.

What odd plants, Julia thought. And so close to the surf, too. How can anything grow there?

Then she stepped closer. And really saw.

No, not plants. Human hands—ten of them, the fingers pale and mummified, crusted with grime and shells.

FIFTEEN

"Gotta give 'em a hand," Alec said, and spewed the same crazy laughter as when they tried to save Kelby down in the bunker, a sound as far away from mirth as Mars from Earth. The meaty grinding of a body trying to turn itself inside-out.

"You're not the first to live here," Moira said, sounding almost awed. "The old versions of you, they're all under there. In the water, too, probably. The bones, at least. We think this facility's been operational for a decade or more."

"What happened to them?" Julia whispered. Everything between her mouth and stomach felt stuffed with concrete.

Moira shrugged. "We don't know. We found the same thing at the other facilities, but we didn't want to dig them up. Maybe they—you—don't have long lives. Sorry, but that might be true. Or else you were... culled."

"Disposable people," Alec said, pausing from his laughter to take a long, shaky breath. "So convenient."

Julia felt like her knees were missing, her legs a pair of stilts about to topple down. She reached out for something to hold, but her hands swept through empty air and so she sank down, down, until her shins rested on the cool sand. It had only taken a boar attack and a hostage situation and a skull-fucking and a mass grave full of clones, but her mind felt ready to well and truly snap. It was an almost physical sensation, a ghost pressure building up at the top of her spine, and behind it was a screeching void, a nonsense world where nothing mattered.

Which sounded pretty good, come to think of it.

No: focus.

FOCUS.

FOCUS.

She stared at those dry fingers poking from the sand, the fingernails cracked, the skin crusted with dirt. Small cuts along the palms and wrists, but no sign of blood. No rot. Weird. Her mind a little clearer now, her breathing easier. Green out, blue in. Blue, blue, blue.

A sharp click echoing off the dunes. Oh shit. Julia slapped her hands over her ears, ready for the sonic blast of the bunker's wilderness speakers. Who would speak in that epic boom? The recruiter, telling them to return underground to their doom? Or perhaps Kurt, not nearly as dead as he looked, begging them to help him? Or maybe it was Kelby returned from the dead yet again, ready to share more thoughts on humankind's deep history.

But the voice, when it came, was barely louder than the wind. And familiar. It sounded like Alec, but trembled in a way that suggested great age:

"The intruder is correct. Our cloning program was originally developed for the military—a very lucrative contract. They asked for certain... enhancements."

Alec twisted on his heel, snarling in confusion. "What the hell? That sounds like me."

"It is you," Moira said. "What did I just tell you?"

I can't deal with this, Julia thought. All these men thrusting around their literal and metaphorical dicks around. Babbling nonsense about government and cryptocurrency and clones. None of that matters to the beach and these dead hands poking from it. None of that matters to the birds or the boars or the rocks.

She spun on her heel, unsure of where to direct her complaint. They had probably inserted those speakers along the entire coast. "If I'm a clone," she said. "Whatever happened to the original me?"

Alec jabbed his cane at the eastern horizon, where a black speck had appeared, hovering above the water. "Problem," he announced.

"I don't know what happened," the older Alec said, sounding tired and old. *"After I went to Kyiv, we... lost touch. You never had a big presence on social media. I tried finding you, but I couldn't."*

Probably because I didn't want to be found, Julia thought. Because enough is enough after a certain point, right? You move on. I mean, unless you make a couple billion dollars. Then you don't have to move on. Then you can spend your money creating a weird little fantasy world where your clone and your ex-girlfriend's clone can sit around and—talk? Fuck for the cameras' amusement? Relive all the old arguments?

"You wanted to hear me say it," Julia told the sand.

"Say what?" The voice inviting her, practically begging her.

"That I love you. That's why you unlocked the gun, right?"

"Yes. And I realized then, I've finally gotten it right." A drawn-out sigh. *"Gotten you right. After so much tweaking."*

A low buzzing as the black speck moved across the ocean, growing into a shape with wings and fins, a bulbous payload dangling from its belly. Its motor must have been a powerful one because she could feel its rumble from here. As it circled overhead, she saw the payload wasn't a missile but a steel container maybe six feet long.

Moira bared her teeth and scooped up a smooth stone, gripping it as if ready to throw.

"Yeah?" Alec shouted at her. "You think that'll work?"

The drone descended to the shoreline, its jets blasting the breakers into clouds of spray and sand. As it hovered eight feet in the air, the container hinged open like a jaw, revealing a glowing blue interior lined with soft foam, like a bed. Above the rumble, she heard a shrill mechanical whine, like a smaller engine gearing to life.

"Come with me, Julia," older Alec boomed from the drone. *"Come with me and we'll finally have our best lives together. It'll be so cool."*

The ghost pressure in her skull gave way. It felt like a soft pop. But instead of screeching insanity she felt calm, clear. It was wonderful. She walked toward the machine, swiping away Moira's hand as she passed, ignoring Alec's look of marvelous confusion. She stopped at the edge of the drone's pummeling downdraft, the wind slapping at her hair, and said, "You're so full of shit. Always were."

"Excuse me?"

"This wasn't a healthy relationship." She turned to the Alec she remembered, expecting to see his trademark wounded-puppy look, but he seemed calm. He nodded for her to continue.

"I loved you," she told him. "I loved you despite everything, and I guess I thought that was enough to cover for everything else, but it's really not. Love is great, yeah, okay, but it's also blind. It can take you where you don't want to go. Obvious, right? Except you never learned that, Alec. And I never learned that, either. Shame on me. I was too blind, and it cost me too many years of my life."

She felt full of blessed blue.

And totally free, despite all evidence to the contrary.

The drone clicked, panels on each wing unfolding to reveal a line of gray barrels. The metallic thud of ammunition loading. *"Whatever,"* the drone announced. *"Climb into the pod. Our love story isn't over yet."*

That shrill whine kept building. It wasn't coming from the drone. A flicker to Julia's right, on the pathway leading to the top of the hill. A pale figure scrambling down the rocks, its hands clutching a blurred metal sword—no, not a sword. A chainsaw.

The figure stumbled into the cove, its body smeared thickly in dark gore glittering with a thousand tiny shards of glass. An iridescent and bloody figure plucked from the depths of the underworld, focused on a terrible mission. It set the smoke-spewing chainsaw on the grass and wiped at its face with the back of its hand, sloughing away a masklike crust of blood to reveal Kelby's wild eyes.

Kelby picked up the chainsaw again. "Came through the skylight," he told Julia. "I know what's what my ancestors would have done, because it's the hard way, the way that challenges…"

Before she could say anything, Kelby's attention shifted to the drone. "You're an affront to the sweep of evolution," he told it, his voice piercing the roar of engines.

"You've demonstrated perseverance," the drone said. *"What would it take to bring you onboard? Stock?"*

The mess made it impossible to see if the five bullet-holes had healed, but Kelby seemed lively as he lurched toward the drone, which whined as it pivoted around, a red laser blazing from its nose. Kelby laughing hysterically above the chainsaw's growl as he advanced, the crimson light glittering off the bits of glass.

"Fuck," Alec said, "he looks just like me."

You're just realizing this now? Julia wanted to ask him, but a growing part of her sensed those were the wrong words for this ultimate moment. She said, "I'm sorry for how all this went down—"

Kelby's chainsaw bit into the underside of the drone, showering bright sparks. Moira screamed and threw herself onto the dirt, but as the drone veered to the left, black smoke boiling from its engines, Julia realized the earth had no reason to protect them. Despite his pretentious babbling, Kelby might have been right about one thing— humanity in its current state was an anomaly, either too smart or too dumb to live. As the drone's batteries cooked off in a supernova of heat and light, making her every cell and molecule sing with fire, she had a microsecond for a final thought: At least she wouldn't have to listen to anyone else's bullshit.

NICK KOLAKOWSKI is the Derringer- and Anthony- nominated author of 'Payback Is Forever,' 'Absolute Unit,' and 'Boise Longpig Hunting Club,' as well as the 'Love & Bullets' trilogy of novellas. He lives and writes in New York City. Visit him virtually at nickkolakowski.com.

Printed in Great Britain
by Amazon

25832222R00079